Who goes here?

Bob Shaw was born in Belfast in 1931 and had a technical
education which led to several years' work in structural design
offices in Ireland, England and Canada. At the age of
twenty-seven he escaped into public relations. Since then he
has worked as a journalist, a full-time author and as press officer
for an aircraft firm. Married with three children, Bob Shaw's
hobbies – apart from writing – are reading, crafts, and 'sitting
with my feet up while drinking beer and yarning with kindred
spirits'. He sold his first science fiction story to the *New York
Post* when he was nineteen, and is now the author of several
novels and many short stories. His books include *The
Two-Timers, Other Days, Other Eyes, The Palace of Eternity,
One Million Tomorrows, Tomorrow Lies in Ambush, Cosmic
Kaleidoscope, A Wreath of Stars, Medusa's Children* and
Orbitsville which won the British Science Fiction Award for
the best novel of 1975 – all published in Pan.

Previously published by
Bob Shaw in Pan Books

The Two-Timers
The Palace of Eternity
One Million Tomorrows
Other Days, Other Eyes
Tomorrow Lies in Ambush
Orbitsville
Cosmic Kaleidoscope
A Wreath of Stars
Medusa's Children

Bob Shaw

Who goes here?

Pan Books London and Sydney

First published 1977 by Victor Gollancz Ltd
This edition published 1979 by Pan Books Ltd,
Cavaye Place, London sw10 9PG
© Bob Shaw 1977
ISBN 0 330 25609 2
Printed and bound in Great Britain by
Hazell Watson & Viney Ltd, Aylesbury, Bucks

chapter one

'You feel better now, don't you?' The pretty technician-nurse smiled at Peace as she leaned across and removed the terminals from his forehead. She had coppery hair and her fingernails were manicured to the perfection of rose petals. 'Tell me how you feel.'

'I'm fine,' Peace said unthinkingly, then realized it was true. He was aware of tensions fleeing from his body, being driven out by the warm sense of ease which was spreading downwards from his brain. Relaxing into the skilfully contoured chair, he looked around the gleaming surgery with benign approval. 'I feel *great*.'

'I'm so glad.' The girl placed the medallion-like terminals and associated leads on top of a squat machine and pushed it away on noiseless casters. 'You know, I get a lot of personal satisfaction through helping people like you.'

'I'm sure you do.'

'It's a kind of . . .' She smiled again, shyly. 'I guess the word is fulfilment.'

'I'll bet it is.' Peace gazed happily at her for a moment, then a stray thought obtruded. 'By the way,' he said, 'what exactly have you done for me?'

'Well, damn you!' she snapped, her face growing pale with anger. 'Thirty seconds you waited before you started asking your bloody stupid questions. Thirty seconds! How much personal satisfaction and fulfilment is a girl expected to cram into thirty seconds?'

'I . . . Wait a mo . . .' Peace was so shocked by her abrupt change of attitude that he found difficulty in speaking. 'I only asked . . .'

'That's right – you only asked. You couldn't simply accept my gift of happiness and be grateful, could you? You had to start checking up on things.'

'I don't understand,' Peace pleaded. 'What's going on here?'

'Come on, buster – *out*!' The girl marched to the door of the surgery, flung it open and spoke to somebody in the next room. 'Private Peace is ready for you now, sir.'

'There must be some mistake,' Peace said, getting to his feet. 'I'm not a private. I'm not in the . . .'

'You want to bet?' the girl said nastily as she pushed him into the adjoining room and slammed the door. His bewildered eyes took in the details of a square office whose walls were decorated with militaria and a large banner of midnight blue on which were embroidered, in silver, the words: SPACE LEGION – 203 Regiment. There was a single desk, behind which was seated a pudgy man wearing the uniform of a Space Legion captain. The blue carpet featured the Space Legion crest, and the various items of office equipment around the room, including the tubs which held ornamental plants, were similarly stencilled or engraved. Nodding a silent greeting, the captain waved Peace into a chair which had 'Space Legion' woven into the fabric of the back and cushion.

'What is this place?' Peace demanded.

'Would you believe,' the officer's gaze flicked around the room, 'the headquarters of the YWCA?'

The sarcasm missed Peace by several light years. 'That woman in the next room called me a private,' he said anxiously.

'Pay no attention to Florence – she gets a bit edgy. The frustrations of the job, you know.'

Peace sighed with relief. 'For a minute I thought I'd done something stupid.'

'No, you haven't done anything stupid. Not in the slightest.' The pudgy man began to scrutinize his fingers with great care, as though taking inventory. 'I'm Captain Widget – the local induction officer for the Space Legion.'

'When I said I thought I had done something stupid,' Peace said, alarm bells clamouring in his mind, 'I meant something like joining the Space Legion.'

Widget lowered his face into his hands, and his shoulders quivered slightly. He remained that way for perhaps a minute, during which Peace stared at the top of his head with growing concern, then he straightened up, apparently making a great effort to bring himself under control.

'Warren,' he said, 'may I call you Warren?'

'That's my name,' Peace said noncommitally.

'Thank you. Warren, doesn't the idea of being in the Legion appeal to you?'

Peace gave a hoot of derision. 'Are you kidding? I've heard all about that – getting shipped all over the galaxy, getting shot at, getting burned up, getting frozen up, getting ate up by monsters, getting . . .' Peace stopped speaking as his suspicions crystallized into certainty that something awful had happened. 'Why should I do anything as crazy as joining the Legion?'

'You've no idea?'

'Of course not.'

'There you are, then!' Widget said triumphantly. 'There you are!'

'Captain, what are you talking about?'

'Let me put it this way, Warren.' Widget leaned across his desk and, unaware that he had placed one of his elbows in a well-used ashtray, fixed Peace with an intense stare. 'Back in the old days – three or four hundred years ago – why did men join the French Foreign Legion?'

'I don't want to play games with you, Captain.'

'Why did they join, Warren?'

'To forget,' Peace said peevishly. 'Everybody knows that, but I . . .'

'And today, Warren, why do men join the Space Legion?'

'To forget – but I haven't got anything I want to forget.'

'Not any more you haven't.' Widget leaned back in his chair, satisfied he had made his point. 'You've forgotten it.'

Peace's jaw sagged. 'This is stupid. What have I forgotten?'

'If I told you that it would spoil everything,' Widget said reasonably. 'Besides, I don't even know what was on your mind when you came in here thirty minutes ago. The Legion respects a man's privacy. We don't ask embarrassing questions – we just hook you up to the machine, and ... bleep! ... it's all gone.'

'Bleep?'

'Yes. Bleep! The crushing burden of guilt and shame is lifted from your soul.'

'I . . .' Peace delved into his memory and found he had no recollection of having walked into the recruiting office. A smothering sense of panic developed within him as he discovered he had no memories at all of a previous life. It was as if he had been created, conjured up out of thin air, a few minutes earlier in the surgery next door.

'What have you done to me?' he mumbled, tentatively pressing his head with his fingertips as though it was a puff-ball which could cave in at the slightest touch. 'I can't remember anything! No past life! No childhood! No nothing!'

Widget raised his eyebrows. 'That's unusual. The machine usually blanks out the previous day or two in their entirety – because of neuro surge – then it becomes selective to take out specific memories. If you can't remember anything at all you must have been a hard case, Warren. Everything you ever did must have been rotten.'

'This is terrible.' Peace was unable to keep a quaver out of his voice. 'I can't even remember what's-her-name – my mother.'

'That makes me feel a lot better,' Widget said. He sat

upright and the curvatures of his well-padded face firmed out and became shiny as he smiled. 'It really churns me up when I have to reorientate nice young men – clean-cut boys who perhaps made only one mistake in their whole lives – but you're different. You must have been *evil*, Warren.

'It's a good thing for you that you don't have to spend years of hard soldiering trying to wipe out the memories of your guilty past, because you'd probably have never made it. It's a good thing for you we've reached the stage where memories can be electronically erased, and that the Legion is prepared to accept you and . . .'

'Shut up!' Peace bellowed, overwhelmed with fear and the urge to find a quiet place where he could concentrate on forcing his brain to do all the things normally expected of it. He rose to his feet. 'I've got to get out of here.'

'I can understand that desire,' Widget said gleefully,' but there's a snag.'

'What is it?'

Widget picked up a sheet of pale blue paper. 'This contract – it binds you to serve in the Legion for thirty years.'

'You know what you can do with that,' Peace sneered. 'I'm not going to sign it.'

'But you've already signed it,' Widget said. 'Before we put you on the machine.'

'I did *not*.' Peace shook his head emphatically. 'What are you trying to pull here? I can't remember anything about myself, but there's one thing I do know, and that is that I would never ever, not in a million years, never ever sign a thing like that, so you can . . .' His voice faded away as Widget pressed a button on a control panel built into his desk and a moving image glimmered into existence on the wall behind him. It depicted a tall young man with a doll-pink face, wide mouth, blue eyes and blond hair which was fashionably thinned above the forehead. Peace had difficulty in recognizing himself at first, then he realized it was because – in the picture – he was a caricature of despair. His eyes were dull and broody, his mouth was turned down at the corners, and his whole drooping, defeated posture suggested a spirit which had broken under some unguessable load.

As Peace watched, his other self sagged into a chair at a table, picked up a pen and signed a pale blue document which was recognizably the same as the one now in Widget's hands. Florence, the technician-nurse, appeared and led an obedient Peace away as would a zoo-keeper attending to a sickly chimp. The images faded from the wall.

'You should see your face!' Widget put a hand over his mouth and nostrils and gave a prolonged snort of amusement. 'Boy, I'm really enjoying this. I'm going to feel good all day after this.'

'Let me see that paper,' Peace said, reaching for the document.

'Certainly.' There was a curious light, which might have been a gleam of anticipation, in Widget's eyes as he handed the sheet across the desk.

'Thank you.' Peace looked at the contract only for as long as it took to satisfy himself that he had actually signed it and that it was printed on ordinary paper instead of indestructible plastic. He held it up by one edge, pinched it between his forefingers and thumbs with an extravagant flourish, and made ready to rip the sheet in half.

'Don't tear that,' Widget snapped. There was a clear note of command in his voice, but he remained at ease and made no attempt to retrieve the document. The glow in his eyes seemed brighter.

Peace gave a contemptuous sniff and tried to pull the sheet apart. A painful and nauseating sensation, like somebody briskly scrubbing the surface of his brain with a rough towel, filled his cranium – and his fingers refused to move.

Widget pointed at the desk. 'Set the paper down there.'

Peace shook his head, but in the same instant his right hand leapt forward and placed the sheet exactly where Widget had indicated. He was staring at his hand, shocked by its treachery, when Widget spoke again.

'Do me an imitation of a rooster.'

Peace shook his head and began crowing at the top of his voice.

'With actions.'

Peace shook his head and began stalking around the office, flapping his elbows.

'That's enough,' Widget ordered. 'I'm tempted to say don't call us, we'll call you – but perhaps farmyard impressions aren't your forte.'

'Captain,' Peace said weakly, 'what's going on here?'

'Had enough, eh?' Widget discovered the cigarette ash on his elbow and spent a minute brushing it off before pointing at the empty chair. 'Sit down there and read your contract, with special attention to Clause Three. The whole thing is written in ultra-simplified language that even a moron can understand, but feel free to ask any questions you want.'

Peace sank into the chair and picked up the contract. It had been imperfectly duplicated from a typescript, and said:

Space Legion
Thirty* Year Service Contract

for Volunteer Rankers

1 I, Warren Peace, citizen of Earth, agree to serve as a private soldier in the Space Legion for thirty* years, and to accept all conditions of service.

* The figure of thirty given here may be taken to read as forty**; depending on the Space Legion's manpower requirements thirty years from the signing of this contract.
** The figure of forty given here may be taken to read as fifty or

2 I enter this Covenant willingly, and without coercion, in return for psychological adjustment – namely, electro-psycho engram erasure – performed by a suitably qualified Medical Officer of the Space Legion.

3 I also agree, in the interests of efficiency, to standard electro-psycho response conditioning.

(signed) Warren Peace
Date: 10th day of November, 2386 AD

Peace set the contract down with a pounding sense of dismay. 'It's obscene,' he said simply. 'It's like something a used car dealer would dream up.'

Widget shrugged. 'You signed it.'

'What was I *thinking* about?'

'That's between you and your conscience,' Widget said primly. 'The point is, you signed it.'

'It would never hold up in a court of law,' Peace challenged, gathering what remained of his strength of mind. 'Why, it doesn't even specify Earth years, and there's no ...'

Widget held up a plump hand. 'Forget all that stuff, Warren – you won't be taking any legal action.'

'Who says so?'

'Clause Three says so.'

Peace leaned forward and checked the relevant wording. 'What's all this about "standard electro-psycho response conditioning"?'

'I thought you'd never ask.' The look of malicious enjoyment returned to Widget's round face as he tapped a small lump protruding from his throat, just above his collar. 'Do you know what this is?'

'It looks like a cyst. I wouldn't worry about it.'

'It isn't a cyst, and I'm not worried – because nearly

sixty years or any other number the Supreme Command of the Space Legion may decide upon if current longevity research proves successful.

every officer in the Space Legion has one just like it.'

Peace shrank back. 'Is there an epidemic?'

'Don't be so damn stupid, man.' Widget paused to re-assemble his smile. 'This is a surgically-implanted Mark Three command enforcer. It adds certain harmonics to my voice – harmonics to which every legionary from the rank of NCO downwards is conditioned to respond with absolute, unthinking obedience. Have you got the picture?'

'I don't believe it,' Peace breathed, aghast. 'Even the Legion wouldn't be allowed to go that far.'

Widget sighed and glanced at his watch. 'Do the rooster impression again – and for God's sake try to get the neck movements right. Last time you were more like a dromedary.'

'I refuse,' Peace said as he left his chair and high-stepped across the office, flapping his elbows and darting his head this way and that in search of worms.

Widget folded his arms and made himself comfortable. 'Let me know when you've had enough.'

'You don't leave a fellow much dignity,' Peace crowed in protest. He essayed a short flight which ended disastrously in a clump of Sirian sparkle plants.

'Dignity you want? It's lucky for you I'm straight.' Widget's eyes flickered ominously. 'This is nothing to what . . .'

'All right, I give in,' Peace said. 'I'm convinced.'

'In that case you can sit down again while I explain the basic terms of service.' Widget stared at the ceiling until Peace had resumed his seat. 'Cigarette?'

Peace nodded gratefully. 'I'd love one.'

'I'm talking about your cigarettes, Warren. Get them out.'

Peace took a pack of Selfigs from his jacket pocket and offered them across the desk.

'I'll get rid of these for you,' Widget said, snatching the whole pack. 'Rankers aren't permitted to smoke during basic training.' He took out a cigarette for himself, puffed it into life, and dropped the others into a drawer.

'Thanks.' Peace stared wistfully at the ascending smoke and wondered how long he had been a tobacco addict. The strength of his craving suggested it had been some time, but his memory held no details. It was disconcerting to find a complete blank where the stored experience of a lifetime ought to be, but – assuming Captain Widget had been right in what he said earlier – he could be better off not knowing what sort of person he really was. His best plan might be to write off the past and accept whatever his new life in the Legion might bring. After all, there was bound to be a great deal of adventure and travel.

'. . . conditions of service are absolutely standard,' Widget was saying. 'The pay is ten monits a day, and . . .'

'An hour,' Peace corrected. 'You meant ten monits an hour.'

'I mean exactly what I said. Don't argue with an officer.'

'Pardon me,' Peace said heavily. 'It must be my lack of memory playing tricks – I thought slavery had been abolished ages ago.'

'You really are a hard case, aren't you?' Widget gazed at him with growing dislike. 'You know, if it wasn't for the fact that it's totally impossible, I'd give you back your memory and leave you to the mercy of the police. You don't deserve the Legion.'

'All I said was . . .'

'Private Peace!' Widget's mouth twitched with anger. 'I see I'm going to be forced to sap you.'

Peace stared at him in alarm. 'Are you allowed to strike a private soldier?'

'SAP stands for Self Administered Punishment,' Widget explained with a vindictive glint in his eyes. 'And I think we'll begin with the good old Bilateral Mamillary Compression and Torsion, otherwise known as the tweak.'

'Wait a minute,' Peace said apprehensively. 'Perhaps I was a little out of line just now. Perhaps...'

'Grasp your nipples between forefingers and thumbs,' Widget ordered.

'Look, can't we behave like sensible adults?' As he spoke, Peace opened his jacket and gripped his nipples through the thin material of his shirt.

'On the command of "tweak" squeeze as hard as you can, at the same time contra-rotating nipples through an angle of approximately two radians,' Widget said, his face stern. 'If you're not familiar with circular measurement, ninety degrees will do.'

'Captain, I'm sure you don't really want to degrade both of us in this...'

'*Tweak!*'

Peace gave a yowl of agony as his hands, obeying his electro-psycho conditioning, carried out the order with what seemed to him an unnecessary vigour. 'You've done it,' he reproached as soon as he could trust his vocal chords. 'You've degraded both of us.'

'I can live with it,' Widget said comfortably. 'Now, I think we were discussing money – how much have you got?'

Peace put his hand in his pocket and produced a slim wad of notes. 'Looks like about two hundred monits.'

'Lend it to me, Warren.' Widget held out his hand. 'I'll pay you back next time I see you.'

Unable to refuse, Peace surrendered the thin sheaf. 'Please don't think I'm implying anything, Captain, but is there any chance of your ever seeing me again?'

'Very little, but you never know your luck. It's a small galaxy, after all.'

Peace considered making a wry comment, but was dissuaded by the painful tingling he could still feel on each side of his chest. He listened in silence to the rest of a brief induction lecture, and then – shorn of cigarettes, money, dignity, and all knowledge of his previous life – he obediently marched out of Captain Widget's office to begin his thirty, forty or fifty years as a ranker in the Space Legion.

chapter two

Peace found himself standing with six other youngish men in a corner of a large hall. All were wearing plastic name badges, and they were gathered in a tight apprehensive group within a small enclosure somebody had set up using portable stanchions linked by rope. Peace examined his surroundings with some curiosity.

The hall was divided into two equal parts by a long counter surmounted by a mesh screen reaching up to the bare, sloping rafters. Lighting strips near the apex glowed a dismal green amidst the tendrils of November fog which had crept in from outside. The more distant tubes were so dimmed by vapour that they resembled rods of luminous ice. Beyond the screen were rows of storage shelves, and at intervals along the counter sat uniformed clerks. They were as motionless as if they had been petrified by the currents of chill air which swirled on the concrete floor.

'What the hell was the hold-up in there?' The speaker was one of the men closest to Peace, a moody-looking individual whose face would have been blue with beard shadow had it not been for the putty-coloured mottling induced in it by the intense cold. His name badge identified him as Pvt Copgrove Farr.

'Sergeant Cleet told us you'd only be a couple of minutes

in there, but you've kept us waiting half an hour,' Farr continued. 'What was going on?'

Peace blinked at him. 'They took away my memory.'

'We all had things to forget. That's no reason to . . .'

'But you don't understand. I've no memory left – it's all gone.'

'*All* of it?' Farr took a step back and a look of wary respect came into his brown eyes. 'You must have been a real *monster*.'

'Might have been,' Peace said gloomily. 'The trouble is I'll never be able to know.'

'You should have done what I did.' A plump, round-shouldered youth – labelled Pvt Vernon A. Ryan – in a green twinkle-suit nudged Peace in the ribs. 'I wrote my problem down, and I've got it hidden away.'

'What's the point of that?'

'Covers me each way,' Ryan gloated. 'I can't be hauled up for whatever it was I did, and while the heat's dying down I get a lot of free travel, and . . .'

'Wait a minute,' Peace said. 'Is that right? I didn't know you can't be tried for something if your memory of it has been erased.'

'Where've you been all your life? Oh, I forgot . . . you don't know.'

'Do you mean . . . you weren't being tortured by your conscience?'

'I doubt it, but then I'm not like you – there seems to be only one strike against me.' Ryan's button-nosed face radiated a smug happiness. 'I'm only going to stay in this outfit for a month or two – see how it goes – then, when I think the time is right, I'll just peep at my bit of paper and I'll be out. Free and clear. Laughing.'

Ryan's ebullience began to irritate Peace. 'Have you looked at your contract?'

'Of course I've looked at it! That's the whole point, my

friend. It binds me to serve the Legion in exchange for memory erasure, but if my memory happens to come back the deal's off.' Ryan elbowed the swarthy man who had first spoken to Peace. 'Just ask old Coppy, here – he's the one who thought the idea up.'

'Keep your voice down,' Farr said, scowling. 'You want the whole world to know?'

'It doesn't matter if you have to give your memory a quiet boost,' Ryan whispered, winking with one eye and then the other, 'the contract will still be nullified. I tell you, this is going to be more like a paid holiday for me.' He gazed all about him with evident satisfaction, further increasing Peace's annoyance. Several of the men near him nodded in furtive agreement.

'Why are we penned up like sheep?' Peace demanded. He moved one of the lightweight stanchions aside and walked out of the enclosure.

'You shouldn't have done that, soldier,' another man said. 'Sergeant Cleet told us to stay put.'

Peace stamped his feet to ward off the encroaching numbness. 'I'm not worried about any sergeant.'

'You would be if you'd seen him,' Ryan put in. 'He's just about the biggest, ugliest, scariest brute I've ever seen. He's got arms like my legs, his mouth's so big that even when it's shut it's half open, and when he . . .' Ryan's voice died away and some of the colour fled from his cheeks as his eyes focused on a point above Peace's head.

Peace turned and found himself confronted by a vision of dread which, despite the incompleteness of Ryan's description, he immediately identified as Sergeant Cleet. The sergeant was a good two metres tall. He was a pyramid of muscle and bone which began with a skull pointed like a howitzer shell and steadily widened downwards through massive, sloping shoulders, a barrel-like torso and legs which were easily as thick as Peace's waist. The power of these limbs was so great that, regardless of the enormous weight they supported, the whole assemblage moved with a silent, springy gait, appearing to bounce a short distance clear of the floor with every step.

'Wadja say, Peace?' Cleet's voice was a subterranean rumble emerging from the cavern of his mouth, which was every bit as large as Ryan had indicated. It appeared to stretch from ear to ear, and for one horrified moment Peace got the impression that it extended around the back of the sergeant's head, a circular band of lips and teeth on the artillery shell of his cranium.

'I . . . I didn't say anything, Sergeant,' Peace mumbled.

'I'm real glad about that.' Cleet came closer, darkening Peace's field of view with his blue uniform. 'And whyja move my stanchion?'

The fear which arose within Peace joined forces with the shock and despair he was already feeling to produce the sudden realization that he could not go on like this for thirty, forty or fifty years, that he would prefer to die at once and get it over with. And, mercifully, the means for a swift and spectacular suicide had placed themselves before him.

'I didn't move it,' he said. 'I *kicked* it, because it was in my way. Anything gets in my way, I kick it.' He demonstrated his brand-new approach to life's problems by lashing out at the stanchion with his foot and toppling it over. His shoes were thinner than he had realized and the contact with the corner of the square post sent waves of pain racing up his leg, but he stood his ground without flinching and waited for annihilation. Cleet's mouth sagged open with amazement, a process which occurred in stages, like the gradual collapse of a suspension bridge. He took a deep breath, a huge machine fuelling up for some monstrous feat of destruction, then sank to his knees and cradled the fallen stanchion in his arms.

'Wadja do that for?' he whimpered. 'You've scuffed the paint. What's Lieutenant Toogood gonna say?'

'I don't care,' Peace said, taken aback.

'It's all right for you – but I'm responsible for these stanchions.' Cleet raised his eyes in reproach. 'I know your type, Peace. You're nothin' but a bully.'

'Listen . . .' Peace shuffled his feet, partly in embarrassment, partly to ease the throbbing in his injured toe.

'Don't kick me!' Cleet cringed back to what he considered a safe distance before speaking again. 'I'm gonna report you to Lieutenant Toogood, Peace. The Lieutenant will fix you, all right. You'll see. You're gonna be tweakin' yourself from now till Christmas. You'll see. By the time the Lieutenant's finished with you your tits are gonna be upside down. You'll see.' He spun around and hurried off down the hall. His conical form was trembling with agitation and he was visibly springing clear of the floor with every step. The group of recruits watched his departure in silence, then – as if responding to a signal – crowded around Peace, overturning the rest of Cleet's stanchions as they did so.

'I never saw anything like that,' one man said, grabbing Peace's hand and shaking it. 'I thought that big gorilla would eat you, but you had him sized up right from the start. How did you do it?'

'It's a knack,' Peace said weakly. His self-destructive impulse had faded and he was beginning to fear that the moment of recklessness had made the outlook for his future even bleaker than before. 'I wonder what this Lieutenant Toogood's like? If somebody like Cleet is afraid of him . . .'

Ryan eyed the door through which Cleet had vanished. 'I don't like the way things are going, men. I think I'll only stay in the Legion long enough to do the basic training and get a free trip to some other world.' Those near him, still recovering from the mental stress of having looked at Cleet, gave murmurs which indicated they had similar plans.

The realization that he was the only man present who had not had the foresight to prepare an escape route from the Legion depressed Peace even further. In a bid to make some reparation for his bad conduct he began uprighting the fallen stanchions and adjusting the linking rope. He had almost completed the task when there was the sound of approaching footsteps. Looking up he saw a spruce, handsome young officer who had a cigarette in one hand and a sheaf of papers in the other. His red-brown hair was worn in the traditional military style—full in the front and long enough to touch his collar at the back.

'I'm Lieutenant Toogood,' he announced. He paused while the group of recruits – Peace among them – produced an assortment of ragged salutes, bows, curtsies and heel-clicks in their eagerness to show respect, then shook his head.

'You can forget all your preconceived notions about saluting officers,' Toogood said. 'We don't bother with that sort of thing in the 203rd. That's all part of an ancient disciplinary system which was designed to inculcate the habit of complete obedience, and as such it's no longer required. The old time-consuming square-bashing and spit-and-polish nonsense has all been done away with, too – that's good to know, isn't it?'

'Yes, sir.' Sheepish smiles broke out among the recruits.

Toogood tapped the lump of the command enforcer in his throat. 'After all, why should we waste all that time and money when you're already conditioned to the point where if I told you to go and cut your throats you'd dash right out and do it?'

The recruits' smiles abruptly vanished.

'The present system, while greatly superior to the old

methods, places a crushing load of responsibility on your officers. Suppose, for example, that one of you behaved in such a way as to make me lose my temper, and I – unthinkingly, of course – shouted the sort of thing that people sometimes say when they are angry . . . the results could be catastrophic.' Toogood puffed luxuriously on his cigarette for a moment while the imaginations of his audience ran riot. 'Think how awful I'd feel afterwards. Think how awful *you'd* feel.'

The recruits nodded glumly, thinking along the lines Toogood had suggested.

'But I'm not going to burden you with my worries,' Toogood continued magnanimously. 'It's my job to look after you while you undergo basic training here at Fort Eccles, and I want you to think of me as your friend. Will you do that?'

Peace nodded vigorously, along with the others. He made a conscientious effort to see the debonair young lieutenant as a friend, but a not-so-still, not-so-small voice in the back of his mind kept telling him otherwise.

'Things are looking worse,' Ryan whispered in his ear. 'I may not even stay long enough to complete basic training.'

'Now that we know exactly where we stand,' Toogood said, 'which one of you upset Sergeant Cleet?'

Peace considered keeping quiet and remaining within the comradely protection of the group, but there was an immediate return of the sandpapering effect on the surface of his brain. Simultaneously, the group – apparently feeling no desire to go into the comradely protection business – shoved him forward with a collective hand.

Trying to look as though he had advanced of his own accord, he fluttered his fingers and said, 'I did it, sir. Private Peace. I didn't mean to . . .'

'Full marks, Peace,' Toogood interrupted. 'What you did shows courage and a quick grasp of the situation – I think you'll be a useful man in the front line.'

He directed his stern gaze at the other recruits. 'The thing which Peace realized immediately – but which the rest of you were too slow to grasp – is that the non-commissioned officer is an anachronism, a virtually useless appendage in the modern army. In the old days his function was that of enforcing discipline, acting as an interface between officers and rankers. But, now that we have the command enforcer and mental conditioning techniques, corporals, sergeants, warrant officers and all others of that ilk are almost redundant. They still exist to carry out the most menial tasks, but no man is given the rank of sergeant until he has proved he's too stupid or cowardly to serve in any other capacity.'

Toogood drew delicately on his cigarette and his eyes became even harder. 'Looking at you men, my first impression is that – with the exception of Private Peace – the Legion has just acquired a bunch of potential NCOs.'

Stung by the insult, the rest of the group stirred uneasily and Peace, still mindful of their lack of solidarity, was unable to resist giving them a smug glance.

'Don't get too full of yourself, Peace,' Toogood continued, withdrawing his approval. 'Sergeant Cleet has locked himself in the toilets. He's probably crying, which means he'll be good for nothing for the rest of the day – and that throws extra work on to me. I'm going to overlook it this time, but you'd all better remember that being tough on sergeants and upsetting them is misconduct which calls for considerable sapping.

'A few of you may already have been introduced to the tweak, but I assure you it's nothing compared to some of the saps I specialize in.' Toogood smiled unpleasantly through plumes of smoke.

'That settles it,' Ryan muttered to Peace. 'I'm not going to stay in this outfit – I'll take my chances outside with the law.'

'Stop talking and follow me,' Toogood ordered, leading

the way to a table on which sat a square metal box. He removed the lid of the box, revealing a greenish interior glow which showed it was a molecular disintegrator of the type used for domestic garbage disposal. The seven recruits glanced at each other nervously and Toogood's smile broadened into a grin.

'This is the bit I always enjoy most,' he said. 'In every batch of rookies there are always a few smart alecs who think they can beat the system. And how do they plan to beat the system? Why, by hiding little memory-joggers somewhere on their persons. Little notes. Little tape recordings. Microdots.' Toogood was still grinning, but his gaze raked the group like machine-gun fire.

'Listen closely to the following order. Any of you who have such mementos tucked away will now produce them, and – without attempting to read their contents – drop them in here.' He illustrated his command by flicking the stub of his cigarette into the disintegrator. The glow within brightened momentarily as the cigarette end was converted to invisible dust.

Toogood's words were followed by a deathly silence which lasted perhaps three seconds, although it seemed to Peace to go on forever. He glanced at Ryan and Farr. Their faces were horribly contorted and he guessed both men were enduring the agonies of cerebral sandpapering as their wills clashed with their mental conditioning. Finally, Ryan took a small envelope from the pocket of his sparkling green suit and, with trembling fingers, dropped it into the waiting box. Farr did the same with a scrap of paper removed from his left sock, while others in the line fumbled similar items out of their underwear and from beneath wristwatch straps. The disintegrator cast a Mephistophelian glow over Toogood's features as it devoured the souvenirs of forgotten crimes and follies.

'That's better,' he said benignly. 'You'll feel a deep inner peace and contentment now that you've rid yourselves of temptation, now that you know you're fully committed to the Legion. How about you, Ryan? You feel better already, don't you?'

'Yes, sir,' Ryan gritted. For a man who was supposed to be enjoying deep inner peace and contentment he looked strangely ill.

Toogood nodded. 'Again, full marks to Private Peace – he was the only one of you who came here today with the honest intention of devoting his life to the Legion. I like that. Do you come from a military family, Peace?'

Peace blinked at him. 'I don't know, sir.'

'What do you mean you don't know?'

'I don't know what sort of family I come from. My memory's all been wiped out.'

'All of it?'

'Yes, sir. I can't remember anything that happened before I came round in that chair.'

Toogood looked impressed. 'You must have been a *monster*, Peace. Your whole life must have been steeped in crime and guilt.'

'Yes, sir,' Peace said unhappily. Repeated assurances that he had been some kind of Anti-Christ in his former existence were beginning to have a bludgeoning effect on him. He wished Toogood would drop the subject and let him forget that he had nothing to remember.

'It's funny, but you don't look like a monster.' Toogood approached Peace and stared intently into his face. 'Or do you? Wait! I think I . . . Has your picture been in the papers?'

'How would I know?' Peace snapped, losing his patience.

'Don't get prickly with me, Peace.' Toogood tapped the lump on his throat as he spoke. 'Remember this. You're in the Legion now – with no gang of thugs and murderers to back you up.'

'Hold on a minute,' Peace protested. 'I hadn't any gang.'

'How do you know? Can you remember not having one?'

'Ah . . . no.'

'There you are,' Toogood said triumphantly.

Recognizing the same kind of logical ploy that had been used on him by Captain Widget, Peace made up his mind to avoid arguing with officers who had years of practice in dealing with amnesiacs. He glanced hopefully past the lieutenant towards the middle of the hall. Toogood, as though taking the hint, gave orders for the group to pass along the central counter, where they would be issued with uniforms and equipment. Ryan and Farr, recovering their powers of speech, immediately began to whisper recriminations over the failure of their scheme. Peace moved away from them and approached a clerk who was sitting under a sign marked: UNIFORMS.

The clerk examined him with baleful yellowish eyes, went to a rack and returned with a plastic helmet and a smaller cup-like object fitted with narrow elasticated straps. He pushed both items towards Peace through a space in the mesh screen, sat down again and appeared to go into a coma. Peace prodded the hollowed-out artifact and saw that it was an athlete's protective cup.

'Excuse me,' he said. 'What's this?'

Light slowly returned to the clerk's eyes. 'That's your uniform.'

'I thought these things were for ball games.'

'In this case they're for preventing ball games.' The clerk gave an evil leer. 'Some of the species you'll be up against fight real dirty.'

Peace stifled a pang of dread. 'Where's the rest of my uniform?'

'That's it, pal. That's all you get.'

'*What?*' Peace laughed uncertainly. 'A helmet and a cup! That's not a uniform.'

'It is if you join 203 Regiment,' the clerk said.

'I don't understand.'

'You don't understand much, do you?' The clerk sighed in exasperation, made as if to walk away, then leaned across the counter. 'The 203rd is sponsored by Triple-Ess. Right?'

Peace nodded. 'What does Triple-Ess mean?'

'Savoury Shrimp Sauce, you dummy. Don't you know *anything* about the Legion?'

'Not a thing.' Peace lowered his voice and leaned forward until his nose was almost touching the other man's through the wire mesh. 'You see, the machine they hooked me up to in surgery wiped out all my memory.'

'All of it?' The clerk pulled backwards abruptly, his eyes widening. 'You must have been a real . . .'

'Don't say it,' Peace cut in. 'I'm sick of hearing that.'

'All right, pal. No offence intended.' The clerk read Peace's name badge. 'I don't want to cross somebody like you, Warren. Honest. I was only . . .'

Peace silenced him with an upraised hand. 'What were you saying about Savoury Shrimp Sauce?'

'Well, they've been having a bad time lately – ever since it was found that the local shrimps are so full of mercury they get taller on a hot day. Sales have dropped right off, so Triple-Ess have a lot less money to put into the Regiment, and they decided to cut down on uniforms.'

'I didn't know the Legion worked that way.'

'You should've joined 186 Regiment. It's home city is Porterburg, too – the recruiting station's just a few blocks south of here – but it's backed by Stingo Pesticides, and they're loaded these days. You'd have got a nice uniform there, Warren.'

Peace pressed the back of a hand to his forehead, wondering why the news about the Space Legion's commercial orientation should have shocked him so much, and his gaze fastened on the resplendent figure of Lieutenant Toogood. 'The Lieutenant's got a full uniform,' he pointed out. 'And Captain Widget, and Sergeant Cleet.'

'Ah, but they're base personnel, stationed right here in Porterburg,' the clerk said. 'It would be bad for Triple-Ess's image if they were seen going around dressed like bums – but you guys will be shipping out as soon as you finish basic training.'

'I see.' Peace turned to leave. 'Thanks for putting me in the picture.'

'Wait a minute, Warren.' The clerk had developed an air of conspiratorial friendliness. 'What sort of shoes are your wearing?'

'Thin ones,' Peace said, realizing that the pain in his damaged toe had faded only because of the numbing coldness seeping up from the concrete floor.

'They'll be no use in the sort of places you'll be sent to. I tell you what I'll do, Warren. I never met a ranker who'd lost more than three months out of his memory, so 'cause you're kind of special I'll let you have these.' The clerk reached under the counter and came up with a huge pair of red boots with gold heels and toe caps.

'What are they?' Peace said, impressed.

'Genuine Startrooper Sevenleague boots – standard issue when Triple-Ess was at the top of the Dow-Jones ratings. That's the last pair on the whole base, Warren. I've been keeping them to sell to some ranker who had a bit of extra cash, but since Captain Widget took over out there nobody gets through with two cents to rub together. You might as well have them.'

'Thanks.' Peace gathered up the heavy boots, tucked them under his arm with the rest of his uniform, and set off towards another window where he could see men being issued with rifles.

'Wear them in health, Warren,' the clerk called after him. 'As long as it lasts, anyway.'

As Peace was approaching the window Ryan and Farr fell into step beside him. Ryan was looking cheerful again, his eyes gleaming in accompaniment to the sparkling of his green suit. Farr's slate-coloured countenance wore a look of shifty contentment.

'Me and Coppy have worked out a new plan,' Ryan said in a low voice. 'I was a bit worried back there, but everything's okay now.'

Peace was reluctantly impressed by their refusal to accept defeat. 'What are you going to do?'

'It's easy! Me and Coppy have a lot of friends in Porterburg, friends who are bound to know what we did to get into this mess. The first leave we get during basic training we'll go and see them – and get our memories back.'

'Supposing we don't get any leave?'

'We're bound to. Anyway, it wouldn't make any difference – me and Coppy would get over the wall some way. We'll get out. Just wait and see.'

'Good luck.' Peace barely had time to wonder if he too had friends in Porterburg when he found himself at the equipment window. A gleaming weapon, vaguely recognizable as a radiation rifle, was thrust into his hands, and in a few seconds he had been jostled out of the building and into a large quadrangle surrounded by a high wall. It resembled the exercise yard in a prison, except that a blue dinosaur-like creature with a single white spot on its belly had been painted on the brickwork opposite the doorway from which the group had emerged. Iron-grey clouds were pursuing each other across the sky and a sleet-laden wind made the dismal hall the recruits had just quit seem a haven of warmth and good cheer. They put on their helmets and huddled together like sheep while Lieutenant Toogood ascended the steps of a small rostrum.

Peace took the opportunity to kick off his lightweight shoes and slip his feet into the resplendent calf-length red-

and-gold boots which had so unexpectedly come into his possession. They were much too large, the tops gaping open around his rather thin legs, but the stout soles gave excellent protection against the cold. He felt blocky little projections under each of his big toes, which seemed a strange flaw in such expensive footwear, and made up his mind to fix them at the first leisure moment.

'Pay attention, men,' Lieutenant Toogood ordered. 'You are about to begin your basic training.'

'I think I'll go over the wall tonight,' Ryan muttered through chattering teeth. 'I couldn't stand much of this.'

'You've all been issued with standard service rifles,' Toogood continued. 'I want you to point them at the blue silhouette on the wall opposite you and pull the triggers. Proceed.'

Slightly surprised at being allowed to fire a lethal weapon with so little preparation, Peace aimed the rifle at the blue dinosaur and pulled the trigger. A slender purple ray stabbed out of the muzzle and struck the wall several metres above the animal silhouette. As effortlessly as he would have directed a spotlight, he brought the ray down until it was hosing its energy against the target circle on the dinosaur's mid-section. The other recruits did like-wise and flakes of brickwork began to fall to the ground from the glowing circle.

'That's enough – don't waste the batteries.' Toogood folded his arms and waited until the last of the purple rays had faded away.

'Congratulations, men! I take back all the things I said about you earlier – you have all completed your basic training with flying colours. You will now board the personnel carrier for transportation to the nearest war.' He pointed at a blue truck which had entered the yard and was lumbering towards the group.

Ryan, who was standing beside Peace, gave a bleat of

alarm. 'Sir! Please, sir! You can't do this to us, sir,' he shouted. 'I thought the basic training went on for weeks.'

'Why should it?' Toogood said mildly, apparently enjoying himself. 'What more do you need to learn?'

'Well . . .' Ryan looked about him in desperation. 'How about more weaponry? You didn't warn us not to point the rifles at each other.'

'But that goes without saying, Private Ryan – I mean, it's obvious, isn't it?'

'Yes, but . . . How about a toughening-up course, sir? We're all as weak and puny as old ladies.'

'Don't worry about it, Ryan. You're expected to shoot the enemy – not wrestle him. Why do you think we provide rifles in the first place?'

'Yes, but . . .' Ryan fell silent and his lower lip began to quiver.

Toogood put on his now-familiar grin. 'I thought you were pleased about the way we eliminated all the spit-and-polish and square-bashing. It's not as if you were planning to hang around Porterburg and contact your family or friends, is it?'

Ryan's mouth opened and closed silently. Farr sidled in close to him and whispered, 'Don't give up, Vernie. Ask him about the . . .'

'You can bugger off,' Ryan sobbed, stamping his heel on Farr's toes. 'This is all your fault. I shouldn't have listened to you in the first place.'

Farr managed to suppress an exclamation as Ryan's considerable weight came down on his foot, but a wan, thoughtful expression appeared on his face and he moved away. At that moment the personnel carrier rolled to a halt beside the group. To Peace's eyes it looked curiously like an ordinary goods wagon which had been given a coat of Space Legion blue. He examined it closely and thought he could discern, beneath the military crest, an over-painted picture of a bottle of sauce being upended on a plate of shrimps. His scrutiny of the vehicle ended when an automatic door in its side slid open to reveal rows of wooden seats.

'Good luck, men,' Toogood said in a ringing voice. 'And no matter what the years ahead may bring, no matter how far you travel in the service of the Legion, I want you to remember – with affection and loyalty – the happy times and comradeship you found here at Fort Eccles in the class of . . .' he paused to glance at his wristwatch, '. . . ten a.m., November tenth, 2386.'

Peace nodded without conviction and, keeping his voluminous boots on with great difficulty, clambered into the truck to begin the first stage of the journey to an unknown star.

chapter three

The journey from Fort Eccles to the spacefield was uncomfortable.

There were no windows in the passenger compartment of the personnel carrier, which meant the recruits were denied the meagre solace of being able to watch the scenery, and for the most part they maintained a broody silence which was broken only by an occasional moan of despair or an outburst of bickering between Ryan and Farr. One man, with a Latin cast of features and temperament to match, even jumped to his feet with a loud cry of 'Mamma mia!' and began banging his head on the metal wall of the compartment. This action, emotionally cathartic though it may have been, produced such thunderous reverberations – plus showers of rust flakes and condensation from the ceiling – that he was quickly prevailed upon to return to his seat.

In contrast to the obvious misery of his companions, all of whom had been nursing secret hopes of beating the system, Peace began to feel perversely cheerful. Leaving Porterburg and Earth was no wrench for him, because he had no memory at all of his previous life, and the prospect of boarding a starship and voyaging away to another part of the galaxy was both glamorous and exciting. He could not recollect ever having seen a spaceship, but he had no difficulty in visualizing the tall, graceful ships with prows like gleaming spires reaching towards the heavens. And here he was – decked out with a helmet, magnificent boots and a rifle – on his way to the stars, sworn to do battle with the enemies of Earth.

Sitting upright on the hard seat, almost relishing its spartan discomfort, Peace began to feel like a real soldier. The effect would have been more complete had he been given a full uniform to wear in place of his houndstooth check jacket and hose, but he knew it was the calibre of the man within that really mattered. As he glanced down at his clothes Peace was struck by the notion that they might contain some information about his identity. He looked inside his jacket and found that the manufacturer's label had been removed – seemingly proof that his former self had been determined to make a complete break with the past.

What could I have done that was so awful? he wondered as he plucked out the severed threads which had held the label. His curiosity aroused, he began searching his pockets and found that one after another was empty except for a few coins. It appeared that before joining the Legion he had deliberately rid himself of all personal possessions, apart from the money and cigarettes which had been appropriated by Captain Widget. But why? Had he been hiding out from the police?

Peace checked his breast pocket last. As is often the case with such pockets, it was too deep and narrow for this hand to reach the bottom, and he was on the point of abandoning the search when a fingertip touched something smooth and hard. Grunting with the effort, he scrabbled the object up into the light and found he was holding a small toad moulded in blue plastic. He gazed at it in perplexity. The toad must have been pressed from a memory-plastic which was activated by the heat of his hand, for – as he was trying to decide its significance – it gathered its haunches and sprang on to the neck of the recruit in front of him. Whimpering with panic, the man – whose name was Benger – swiped the little creature to the floor and stamped on it, reducing it to a shapeless blob.

'Who's trying to be funny?' Benger demanded, swinging round. 'I'll tear . . . Oh, it's you, Warren.' He gave a sickly smile. 'That was a good one, Warren – you nearly scared the tripes out of me.'

Peace withheld his instinctive apology, deciding to let his fearsome reputation go on smoothing the way for him. 'You didn't have to flatten it, did you?'

'Sorry, Warren. I'll buy you another one first chance I get.'

Peace retrieved the piece of plastic, becoming interested. 'You've seen them on sale somewhere?'

'No, but toys like that can't be too hard to . . .' Benger broke off and a doleful expression appeared on his face as the truck swerved and came to a halt. 'We must be at the spacefield.'

Peace forgot about the destruction of his single personal possession as the compartment's automatic doors began to open, giving him his first glimpse of a bustling interstellar port. He hurried to the door and eagerly looked out, only to experience a pang of disappointment as he discovered he had apparently arrived at a slack period. There were no starships to be seen anywhere on the expanse of frozen mud. A dozen shabby seagulls wandered dispiritedly on the barren ground, emitting raucous cries of disapproval. The sole human presence was that of a Space Legion lieutenant who – judging by the corpse-like pallor of his face – had been awaiting the personnel carrier for some time. He was standing at the entrance to a low, windowless metal building which was about two hundred metres long and had a raised section at each end. Its heavily welded seams gave it the appearance of a hastily constructed air-raid shelter.

'This way, you men,' the lieutenant ordered, opening a steel door. 'In here.'

Peace led a reluctant file of men into the building and discovered that, for a space terminal, it was singularly lacking in amenities. He was in a long narrow room which had a door at each end, transverse rows of benches, and a lone coffee machine. The lieutenant, who remained outside, slammed the entrance door behind them and there followed the sound of bolts clunking into place. A klaxon howled briefly, wringing a fresh chorus of moans from Peace's companions. Puzzled by and slightly contemptuous of their nerviness, he sat down slightly apart from the others and composed himself to wait for the arrival of the spaceship which was to carry him across the oceans of infinity. He was disappointed that the terminal building had no windows through which he would be able to view the great vessel descending from the sky, but consoled himself with the thought that as a legionary he would have lots of other opportunities to admire the tall ships.

Thirty minutes went by before Peace became restless. He toyed with the flattened corpse of his plastic toad, threw it irreverently to the floor, went to the coffee machine and found it was empty, then walked around the room several times, growing more and more impatient. The gloomy torpor of the other recruits, who remained slumped on the benches, served to heighten his annoyance and resentment at being penned up like an animal. Finally, losing his temper altogether, he went to the door by which he had entered the room and tried to throw it open. It refused to move. He slid his hand into a recess in the metal, pressed down on a lever within and began hitting the door with his shoulder.

'Hey, look at old Warren,' somebody said in the background. 'He's pretending to open the door.'

'That's Warren for you,' Benger commented. 'Anything for a laugh.'

'Wait a minute,' cut in another voice, 'I think he's really trying to . . .'

'My God! He's trying to open the door!'

A bench was knocked over and an instant later Peace found himself lying on the floor, with Vernie Ryan sitting on his chest. Another recruit was sprawled across his legs, immobilizing him.

'Sorry to have to do this, Warren,' Ryan said, panting. 'I know a guy like you doesn't care about anything, but the rest of us aren't ready to die.'

'Die? What are you talking about?' Peace found it difficult to speak with Ryan's bulk compressing his ribcage. 'I just wanted to look for our ship.'

Ryan exchanged glances with the onlookers. 'This *is* our ship, Warren. We're in it. Didn't you know we took off half an hour ago?'

'In this tin box!' Peace sneered his disbelief. 'Do I look like an idiot?'

Farr's dark face came into view. 'Which idiot do you mean?'

'That's enough, Coppy,' Ryan said. 'Remember Warren's memory has been wiped out. He knows hardly anything about anything.'

Peace fought for breath. 'I know this isn't a spaceship, that's for sure. It isn't even the right shape.'

'It doesn't have to be any special shape,' Ryan explained. 'It doesn't have to be streamlined – not when it doesn't move.'

'Got you!' Peace said triumphantly. 'You said we took off. How can we take off in something that doesn't move?'

Farr appeared again. 'This boy was in orbit before we started.'

'Lay off him, Coppy.' Ryan looked down at Peace with a kindly, pleading expression on his face, like a junior school teacher giving special attention to a dull child. 'Don't you see, Warren, that a spaceship which moved would never get you anywhere?'

'No, I . . .' In view of Ryan's obvious sincerity, Peace began to doubt his own position. 'Who said so?'

'Albert Einstein, among others. Oh, you could do a bit of local planet-hopping like they did in the old days, but your ship would never be able to go faster than the speed of light, which means it would be pretty useless for interstellar work. The light barrier would see to that.'

'So you get around the light barrier by using a ship which doesn't move?'

'That's it!' Ryan looked pleased. 'You're getting the idea.'

'I am?'

'Of course you are. A brainy character like you . . . Already you'll be asking yourself what a spaceship designer would do if all the conventional forms of locomotion were ruled out.'

'That's right,' Peace admitted. 'That's what I'm asking myself.'

'I knew it! And already your mind will be sifting through the various possibilities . . .'

'Yes, yes,' Peace said, compliantly, feeling the growing excitement of intellectual adventure.

'. . . spurning one unsatisfactory solution after another . . .'

'Yes, yes.'

'. . . until it finally settles on . . .'

'Yes, yes.'

'. . . non-Euclidean tachyon displacement.'

'Oh!' Peace tried to conceal his disappointment. 'Non-Euclidean tachyon displacement.'

Ryan nodded eagerly. 'Which, of course, is just another way of saying instantaneous matter transmission.'

Peace's hopes picked up, but only momentarily. 'If it's instantaneous why have we been sitting around in here for so long?'

'Well, it can't be *completely* instantaneous – that would involve us with the logical absurdity of being in two different places at once. But it's so close to instantaneous that you wouldn't notice the difference.'

'I notice the difference,' Peace said. 'It seems to me that forty minutes . . .'

'Ah, but you haven't thought it through, Warren. We don't complete journeys in one jump.'

'Why not?'

'Because you can't have too great a distance between your transmitting station and your receiving station. Above a certain range there's a loss of fidelity, and a risk of incomplete reception.' A solemn expression flitted across Ryan's face. 'That could be very nasty.'

'So what sort of distance do we transmit across?'

'Two hundred metres.'

'*Two hun...!*' Peace renewed his efforts to wriggle free, but fell back, exhausted.

'I'm sorry, Warren – we can't risk letting you up until you understand that we're out in space and would all be killed if you opened that door.'

'All right,' Peace said in a strangled voice. 'Tell me the rest. Tell me we've got chains of matter transceivers all over the galaxy . . . trillions of them . . . two hundred metres apart.'

'Now you're being silly,' Ryan reproved. 'Just when you were doing so well, too.'

'I'm sorry – I won't argue again. Teach me how it all works.'

'I wouldn't presume to try teaching anything to a well-educated guy like you, Warren. You're working it out for yourself. Remember?'

'Yes, but . . .' Peace gazed up into Ryan's watchful eyes, seeking inspiration. 'Give me a clue, Vernie.'

Ryan glanced at the others, most of whom, Peace was relieved to see, were nodding vigorously. 'All right, then. Tell me what you noticed about this ship when you got down out of the personnel carrier.'

'Let's see,' Peace said, anxious to co-operate. 'It looked like a long, narrow metal box with a sort of low tower at each end.'

'Very good, Warren. Very observant. And how far apart would you say those towers were?'

'About two hundred metres, but I don't see . . .' Peace stopped speaking as he noticed that Ryan's eyes had brightened expectantly. 'Two hun . . .' He broke off again, partly because the idea which had sprung into being in his mind was too preposterous for words, partly because Ryan had begun to bounce encouragingly on his chest, driving the air from his lungs.

'Go on, Warren,' Ryan urged. 'It's a privilege and a pleasure for me to see a first-class brain at work.'

'There's a matter transmitter at the back of the ship,'

Peace said in dazed tones. 'And a matter receiver at the front of the ship. And the ship transmits itself forward two hundred metres at a time. And receives itself.'

'Stand up, Warren.' Ryan's face glowed with vicarious pride as he got off Peace's chest and helped him to his feet. 'I knew you could figure it out for yourself, a bright boy like you.'

'Thank you.' Silent shrieks of disbelief were ringing through every compartment of Peace's mind, but he guessed the penalty for showing his true feelings would be another interlude on the floor. 'Of course,' he said tentatively, seeking a neutral form of words, 'it's not quite as simple as that.'

'You're right there, Warren.' Ryan brushed dust from Peace's clothes. 'I can see your mind is busy delving into the implications of the basic principle.'

Peace nodded. 'Naturally.'

'You're probably delving into stuff that even I don't really understand – stuff about how it's stellar-type condensation of matter around the ship's centre of gravity that produces spatial displacement with every jump, stuff about the need to make one and a half million jumps a second to give an apparent velocity equal to that of light, stuff about the artificial gravity generators . . .'

'Yes – all that kind of thing,' Peace said faintly, turning away and making for the nearest seat. Somewhere along the line he had become convinced of the truth of Ryan's words, and the knowledge that his own body was being torn apart and rebuilt millions of times every second made him feel weak at the knees. *This is terrible*, he thought. The erasure of all conscious memory meant that his world-picture was being formed in his subconscious – and it appeared that his subconscious self was an impractical, romantic twit with no idea of how anything worked in the real universe. His earlier pleasure at being a legionary had been based on the notion of crusading through the galaxy – in one piece – in a beautiful silver ship, not being wafted from star to star as a cloud of particles inside a steel lunchbox. The adjustment was a difficult one to make, and Peace longed for the solace of a cigarette.

'What's the matter, Warren?' Ryan sat down nearby. 'Not feeling so good?'

Peace jumped to his feet to prove there was nothing wrong with him, but he was unable to resist the sympathetic expression on Ryan's plump face. 'Everything's all wrong,' he said. 'I'm dying for a smoke . . . and I didn't know I'd be fighting for a ketchup manufacturer.'

'Please don't mention fighting,' Ryan said, looking apprehensive. 'Anyway, you'll be . . . doing what you said . . . for the Legion. Triple-Ess only kits out the regiment.'

'It's a bit degrading, isn't it?'

Ryan pondered for a moment. 'For the likes of you, perhaps.'

'What do you mean for the likes of me? Having no memory doesn't make me special.'

'All I meant was you weren't cut out to be a ranker, Warren. I can tell from the way you talk you've been to college. You must be a bright boy – not like old Coppy over there. I mean, when you joined the Legion you knew there was no way out. Old Coppy talked me into believing we could duck out any time we . . .'

'College, you say?' Peace turned the new fact over in his mind, but failed to draw any comfort from it. 'From the cloisters to the sauce works.'

'Forget about sauce, will you? Look, would you feel better if things hadn't changed since the seventeenth century and this outfit was called the Duke of Wellington's Regiment?'

'Daresay I would.'

'Right. And would it make any difference that the Duke

who equipped the regiment got most of his money from the revenues of his family estate?'

'No.'

'And what if the Duke's biggest tenant was a sauce factory?'

'That's different,' Peace said, feeling he had been tricked. 'Anyway the Duke of Wellington would have given me a better uniform than this.'

'You look great the way you are, Warren.'

'Think so?' Mollified by the compliment, Peace glanced down at himself and wished he had been blessed with thicker legs or that his red-and-gold boots had been ten sizes smaller.

'No kidding, Warren – you look as smart as old General Nightingale himself.' In his enthusiasm, Ryan turned to Copgrove Farr, who had dropped on to the bench beside him. 'How do you think he looks?'

Farr examined Peace with a lacklustre eye. 'With those legs – like a jaybird standing in two empty shotgun shells.'

'Aw, come on, Coppy – I'd say he's a real Beau Geste.'

'Beau who?'

'You know – Beau Geste.'

Farr's face became darker. 'More like Bo Peep.'

'Now see here!' Peace advanced on Farr, trying to avoid stepping out of his boots as he did so. 'Don't forget who I am.'

'Why not?' Farr said. 'You've done it.'

'I know, but . . .'

'I don't believe you're such a hard case, anyway,' Farr continued, sneering. 'For all we know you've just got a lousy memory.'

Ryan raised a placating hand. 'Look at the way he faced up to Sergeant Cleet.'

'Anybody can do that.' Farr crooked his fingers and a look of savage anticipation appeared on his face. 'The next sergeant I meet I'm gonna . . .' The klaxon blared out suddenly, obliterating Farr's words and causing other recruits to scuttle to their seats.

'Attention, men,' an amplified voice said. 'We have reached the planet Ulpha and are going into the landing phase. If your seat has a safety belt, fasten it and remain seated until the door opens.'

Peace looked down at his bench and noted that it had ring-like anchorages at intervals along the back, but no straps of any kind. A commotion broke out all around him as men, Ryan and Farr among them, scrambled for the few places on other benches where straps were still in evidence. The panic died down momentarily and then flared up again as most of those who had begun securing themselves discovered they had only one strap each and were unable to complete their restraining loops. The Legion's field officers, he decided, would need every last gram of their battle experience and leadership to weld the class of ten a.m. into an efficient fighting unit. He had no relish for the idea of going into combat, but at least it would be a relief to see the reins taken up by the strong hands of a professional commander, a man who had been honed and tempered and toughened by his years in the front line.

The floor lurched gently, the first indication of movement the ship had given, and Peace sat upright, his heart quickening as the ship seemed to drop a few centimetres, like an elevator with a faulty control mechanism coming to rest, and the metal door sprang open. Beyond it was a swirling of blue-white vapours through which came running a humanoid figure with huge black eyes and a short, wrinkled trunk where its nose and mouth should have been. A multiple gasp of fear arose from the watching recruits.

Peace grabbed nervously for his rifle, then realized the dreadful figure was actually a Legion officer whose face

43

was hidden by a gas mask. The officer staggered into the ship and slammed the door behind him, dispersing little whorls of the blue-white mist through the room. He slumped against the door for a moment, breathing heavily, before taking off the respirator and scanning the group with red-rimmed eyes.

'I'm Lieutenant Merriman,' he said in a thin, fluting voice which was in ill accord with the stained and dust-streaked uniform of a front-line veteran. 'You men have arrived just in time – the Ulphans are hitting us with everything they've got.' He paused and knuckled his streaming eyes. 'Where are your respirators?'

'Respirators, sir?' Peace took his athlete's protective cup from his pocket and dangled it by its elasticated straps. 'This is the only extra equipment we got.'

Merriman gave an impatient wave. 'You'll just have to manage without. All of you follow me – we're going into action.'

'But, sir . . .' Even as he spoke, Peace felt the now-familiar sandpapering sensation on the surface of his brain, and knew he was unable to disobey the order. The other ranks shuffled uneasily, faces revealing their mental torment.

'Hurry it up,' Merriman piped, impatience nudging his voice into the falsetto ranges. 'You'll have to be sharper than this when you're fighting for Terra.'

'Excuse me, sir.' Benger held up his hand. 'There must be some mistake – we're from Earth.'

'I know that, you fool.'

Benger glanced around him in perplexity. 'But you just said we'd be fighting for some place I never even . . .'

'Are you trying to be funny?' Merriman moved closer to Benger and read his name badge. 'Give yourself three tweaks, Benger.'

While the unfortunate Benger was administering his own punishment, Peace had time to look more closely at

Merriman and was dismayed to see that, underneath the grease and grime of battle, the lieutenant was a baby-faced youth of about eighteen. He had blue eyes of an idealistic clarity, and girlish lips which were permanently parted to reveal exceptionally large square teeth, and if he had been honed and tempered and toughened by his time in the front line it certainly did not show. Peace was beginning to feel anxious about serving under someone as inexperienced as Merriman when he noticed a tantalizing aroma drifting in the air. He sniffed at it disbelievingly.

'We can't delay any longer.' Merriman gazed critically at his men, who stared back over the rims of their improvised masks. 'It's too bad you don't even have goggles to protect your eyes. That stuff out there really goes for the eyes.'

'Excuse me, sir.' Peace raised a tentative hand. 'It smells like tobacco smoke.'

Merriman nodded. 'Quick work, Peace – that's exactly what it is.'

'Ordinary tobacco smoke, sir.'

'There's no such thing as ordinary tobacco smoke, Peace,' Merriman said impatiently, the ellipse of his mouth changing position slightly with respect to the wall of teeth behind it. 'It all stunts your growth. It's all carcinogenic, and did you know that, weight for weight, nicotine is practically the deadliest poison known to man?'

'It doesn't bother me, sir – I like it.'

'You mean . . . you're a *smoker*?'

'Yes, sir. I think so, sir.'

'Goodness gracious!' Merriman's lips tightened in disapproval and actually succeeded in meeting for an instant, but the outward pressure of the teeth within was too great and after a convulsive twitch his mouth sprang open once more. Peace was reminded of somebody struggling to close the zip on an overfull holdall.

'Goodness gracious!' Merriman repeated, relieving his

anger by what he apparently regarded as strong language. 'A victim of the weed! You'll have no stamina. No wind. What sort of wretches is Terra reduced to sending us?'

'You've said it again, sir,' Benger put in doggedly. 'Are you sure there isn't a mistake? We're definitely from Earth and not from . . .'

'Six more tweaks, Benger,' Merriman snapped without turning his head. 'All right, you men, we've wasted enough time. Follow me!'

He pulled his gas mask up over his face and flung open the metal door. Blue-white smoke wreathed outside, occasionally lit up by orange flashes, and there was the sound of explosions and old-fashioned gunfire. Merriman, quite unnecessarily, windmilled his right arm once in slow motion – a signal which Peace was certain had been culled from twentieth-century war movies, dropped into a crouch and ran forward. His squad of recruits nervously adopted similar attitudes and scuttled along behind him. Ryan, plumply incongruous in his green glitter suit, was snorting with effort before he had taken a dozen paces, and Benger, who was still tweaking himself, kept leaping in the air and emitting yelps of pain.

Peace heard the ship's door clang shut behind him. He glanced back and saw the long metal structure sail up into the sky in a blurred arc described by fast-fading images of itself. In a second it had vanished, leaving him no recourse but to follow his companions into whatever straits a sardonic destiny had prepared for them.

chapter four

At first Peace felt too self-conscious to double himself over, but he was quickly persuaded otherwise by the whine of metal fragments slicing through the air close at hand. He tried creeping after the others, but the roominess of his boots meant that he had a tendency to crawl right out of them, and he was reduced to proceeding in a hunkered down position, giving a grotesque imitation of a Ukrainian dancer. The boots had proved extremely troublesome despite their splendid appearance, and he began to wish he had retained his snug-fitting civilian shoes.

From the lowly position Peace was able to see little of his surroundings, but his squad was moving across open ground which was uniformly covered with a single species of broad-leaved plant. The only agreeable thing about the environment was the abundance of tobacco smoke, and he gratefully inhaled its fragrance while he laboured to catch up on the others. As the minutes went by he began to perspire with his efforts, and there came the realization that this was no localized gas attack. The Ulphans had made a tactical blunder in believing the nicotine-laden smoke would incapacitate all Earthmen, but the scale of their operation suggested they had no need to worry.

Peace risked standing up in an attempt to see the enemy. A warm breeze momentarily lifted the curtain of haze and he glimpsed an undulating plain, covered with the same yellowish vegetation, from which protruded several low conical hills. One of the cones appeared to be glowing a rather pretty shade of pink. Entranced by this first vision of an alien planet, Peace shaded his eyes for a better look, scarcely noticing the abrupt swarming of metal hornets in his vicinity.

'Get down, you fool,' Merriman shouted. 'You're drawing their fire.'

Peace dropped into the cover of the vegetation and churned his way forward to where the rest of the squad had taken shelter behind some fresh earthworks. About twenty legionaries were already huddled there, a few wearing gasmasks, and Peace eyed them with interest. Apart from Lieutenant Merriman, who hardly counted, these were the first combat veterans he had seen, and even the filthiness of their clothing and equipment invested them with a rugged glamour. For their part, the veterans appeared not to notice the arrival of reinforcements. A captain who was with them began striding towards Merriman. He paused as he came close to Peace, and the part of his face not covered by his mask showed unmistakable contempt.

'Why are you crouching there like a frightened rabbit?' His eyes had triangulated on Peace. 'What sort of soldier are you? What has proud Terra come to?'

Peace began to salute, then changed his mind. 'It was Lieutenant Merriman, sir. He told me . . .'

'Don't try to blame an officer of the Legion for your lack of guts,' the captain hissed. 'By Jupiter, you're not fit to live on proud Terra, but I'll make sure you die for her. That's a promise.' He crawled away without waiting for a reply.

'Yes, sir,' Peace quavered to the captain's departing figure.

'Tough luck,' Benger said, approaching on his hands and knees. His expression of sympathy was quickly ousted by one of puzzlement. 'Hey, Warren, where's this Terra these characters keep talking about?'

'How the hell would I know?' Peace was too alarmed by the new turn of events to be interested in the petty worries of others.

'It means Earth,' put in one of the battle-stained legionaries. 'All officers say Terra when they mean Earth. Nobody knows why, but you better get used to it. And the ones that call it proud Terra are the worst.' His eyes flickered meaningfully in Peace's direction.

Peace shivered. 'Do you think the captain meant what he said? Has he got me down on his list?'

'Cap'n Handy won't hold a personal grudge, if that's what you mean.'

'That's a relief. For a minute I thought . . .'

'There's no need for it,' the legionary continued. 'He's going to get the bloody lot of us killed, so he doesn't have to give nobody no special treatment.'

Peace tightened his grip on his radiation rifle, and tried to bolster his courage. 'Some of us mightn't die so easily.'

'If they order you to march straight up to one of those machine gun posts out there, you'll do it just like the rest of us – and you'll die real easy.'

'I can't listen to any more of this,' Benger said faintly. 'I think I'm going to be sick.' He crawled away into the smoke, and there followed sounds which showed his premonition had been correct.

'But it isn't in an officer's own interests to squander his men.' Anxious to get all the information he could, Peace squirmed closer to the legionary. 'Say, where's your name badge?'

'The name's Bud Dinkle, but my badge fell off ages ago – they don't know how to make 'em properly.'

Peace looked down at his own badge and noticed for the first time that the plastic rectangle was held in place by nothing more than a small safety pin and a piece of flesh-coloured surgical tape. The tape was already beginning to lose its adhesion, allowing the badge to hang sideways. He adjusted it to a proper angle and pressed it against his chest, hoping to effect a quick repair.

'That won't help,' Dinkle said. 'They tell you to wear your badge at all times, but they . . .' He paused and gazed stoically at his fingernails until a series of ear-punishing explosions had died away. Peace, almost certain he had heard a short-lived scream amid the clamour, looked nervously about him, but the smoke had grown thick again and he could see only twenty or thirty paces in any direction.

He tugged Dinkle's sleeve. 'How long will the gas attack go on?'

'Gas?' Dinkle began fumbling urgently with his respirator. 'Nobody flaming well told me about gas. What sort?'

'This stuff all around us.'

Dinkle dropped his mask and gave Peace a hard stare. 'You trying to be funny?'

'No. It's just that Lieutenant Merriman said . . .'

'That poop! Didn't he tell you guys the whole planet's like this?'

'The whole planet?'

'It's the standard Ulphan atmosphere.' Dinkle tore up a piece of the ubiquitous yellow vegetation and held it under Peace's nose. 'Sniff that.'

Peace did as he was told. 'Tobacco?'

'Correct, sonny. The entire surface of Ulpha is covered with it, and when you've got all those little volcanoes spreading lava and hot cinders about . . . What's the matter with you?'

'Nothing,' Peace said through cupped hands. 'I didn't expect things to be like this, that's all. Where's the glory? Where's the grandeur?'

'Search me,' Dinkle replied unfeelingly. 'I'm just here to fight a war.'

'But *why*?'

'All I know is the Ulphans started the trouble. The only thing Earth expects from the other worlds in the Federation is that they honour the Common Rights Charter and the Free Trading Pact. That's only fair, isn't it?'

'I guess so,' Peace said, trying to feel reassured. 'What were the Ulphans up to? Slavery? Torture?'

'Worse than that, Warren. They were screwing up the whole Free Trading Pact. Refusing to import their quota of some Earth products.'

An odd inflexion in Dinkle's voice aroused Peace's interest. 'What sort of products?'

'Cigarettes and cigars.'

'Cigarettes? Cigars?'

Dinkle nodded soberly. 'Not only that – they wanted to flood the rest of the Federation with underpriced tobacco.' He scowled in patriotic anger. 'People like that deserve all that's coming to them.'

'But you can see their point of view,' Peace said. 'I mean . . .'

'Who can see their point of view?' Dinkle narrowed his eyes. 'What are you, Warren? A relativist? A greeno?'

'No. At least, I don't think so. What's a greeno?'

'I get it – this is an attitude test,' Dinkle said. 'I thought you didn't sound like an ordinary ranker, Warren, and if I called Lieutenant Merriman a poop just now, I want you to know that, with me, poop's a term of endearment. I call all my best friends poops.' He tapped the legionary next to him on the shoulder. 'Isn't that right, poop?'

The legionary grabbed Dinkle's throat. 'Who are you callin' poop?'

Dinkle tried to fight him off, but the struggle was cut short by an order from Lieutenant Merriman, who directed everybody to gather close to Captain Handy. The men, experienced combat veterans and raw recruits alike, formed a semicircle around the point where Handy and Merriman were sitting with their backs to the low earthen wall. Tobacco smoke floated steadily across the scene and hidden machine guns kept up their peevish snapping. Peace found it difficult to believe that only a few hours earlier he had been safely at home on Earth. He had no idea what had been happening to him before he joined the Legion, but anything had to be better than his current predicament.

'Captain Handy wants to deliver a personal message to all of you,' Merriman fluted, cautiously raising his mask a little. He smiled, which meant that the ellipse of his mouth elongated to show one extra tooth at each end. 'I know that, as I do, you respect Captain Handy as one of the finest officers in the entire Legion, and for that reason you'll regard it as an honour and a privilege – just as I do – that he has found time to come here and direct this phase of the battle in person with all the superb leadership, skill and courage for which he is justly renowned.'

Handy nodded his agreement with everything that had been said, and tapped the cyst-like lump of the command enforcer on his throat. 'Men, it may come as a surprise to you to learn that I don't like wearing this thing. Not only is it an expensive contraption, but I happen to believe it is totally unnecessary. I know that, given the chance, each and every one of you would be prepared to lay down his life for proud Terra without any electronic coercion.'

'We've had it,' Dinkle whispered gloomily to those beside him. 'This is where he starts blowing off about the daunting psychological impact on the enemy of seeing proud Terra's warriors marching line abreast and unafraid into the mouths of the cannons.'

'Keep quite,' Peace said. 'No commander would be so stupid.'

'It's the only tactic Cap'n Handy knows – he's famous for it.' Dinkle punctuated his words by spitting savagely, realized too late that his foot was in the way, and began wiping saliva off his toecap. 'I tell you, we're buggered.'

'. . . going to level with you men,' Handy was saying. 'Things are going badly in this sector. Proud Terra's thin red line is too thin and too . . . er . . . red. I can't promise you a quick victory like the one we had on Aspatria. But we've got one tremendous advantage, one great weapon the enemy doesn't possess – and that is our invincible spirit. These Ulphans are an undisciplined, cowardly rabble. The only way they can bring themselves to fight is by skulking under cover and firing from behind rocks.' Handy paused to register his contempt for what he obviously regarded as a lack of common decency.

'So what we're going to do in this sector is to use our invincible weapon, our moral superiority, our spirit. The Ulphans expect us to fight in the same lily-livered way that they do – but we're going to surprise them by going straight in. Straight in with our heads held high and our banners waving. Can you imagine the daunting psychological impact of seeing proud Terra's warriors marching line abreast and unafraid into the mouths of the cannons?'

His audience shifted uneasily as their imaginations went to work.

'There'll be casualties, of course,' Handy went on, perhaps disappointed by a lack of favourable response. 'There may even by heavy casualties before the enemy turns tail and flees, but the annals of military history are full of similar glorious episodes. Just think of the charge of the Light Brigade.'

Benger raised his hand. 'Sir, I saw a movie about the charge of the Light Brigade. Didn't they all get killed? Wasn't it all a big mistake?'

'Ten tweaks, Benger,' Merriman ordered, his mouth sliding about with displeasure like a spotlight playing on a backdrop of teeth. Glad of the diversion, most of the audience turned to watch and listen to Benger sapping himself, but at that moment a shell exploded close by and they threw themselves flat. The shrapnel from it chittered through the vegetation, and when Peace sat up again he noticed that one man, only a few metres from him, was writhing in silent agony. Two others with Red Cross armbands picked him up and retreated as quickly as they could.

'I hope you all saw that,' Captain Handy said crisply. 'I hope you all saw that and were comforted and encouraged. Thanks to their refusal to stay in the progressive interstellar society of the Federation the Ulphans are forced to rely on their obsolete projectile weapons. You soldiers of proud Terra, on the other hand, are armed with the finest radiation rifles available. Weapons of unlimited range and unsurpassed accuracy, each one worth a dozen of the enemy's pathetic machine guns.

'Now I want you to go out there and use them. Use them well. Go out there, walking proud and tall and unafraid, and kill as many dirty Ulphans as you can and make the galaxy a fit place for all right-thinking beings to live in, that is, in which to live ... er ... in.'

Lieutenant Merriman, seemingly oblivious to the fact that it was unnecessary, paddled his hands in the manner of a man damping down applause. 'Men, I'm sure that, just as I am, you're inspired and uplifted by those words from Captain Handy. But now, men, the time for talking is over – it's time to go over the top.'

'It's all right for him,' Peace muttered, an icy coldness growing in his stomach. 'While we're going over the top he'll be back here.'

'No, he won't,' Dinkle said, tightening the chinstrap of his helmet. 'Those young loonies who've been through military academy lead all the charges. That's why they don't last long – I've never seen one older than about twenty.'

'What makes them do it?'

'Tradition, I guess. They're all the same – crazy as loons.'

'That's great,' Peace said bitterly as he watched Lieutenant Merriman get to his feet, give his windmill signal with one arm and scramble over the bank of churned earth. The sound of gunfire intensified immediately. Peace thought briefly about crouching down and refusing to move, but the invisible wire brushes went to work inside his head and, before he really knew what was happening, he was on his feet and running towards the Ulphan positions.

As before, the excessive roominess of his footwear made progress difficult and he saw the rest of his unit disappear into the smoke ahead of him. He curled his toes in an effort to hold the boots in place, and one of the odd interior projections he had noticed earlier moved downwards slightly. An instant later he was sailing through the air, like an Olympic ski-jumper making a fantastic leap, borne by the upwards pressure of his boots. Too astonished to cry out, Peace fought to maintain his balance and to keep his legs together as the boots tried to go off in different directions, threatening to pull him apart. They carried him, unseen, in a precarious parabola far above the heads of his companions, and for a few seconds he lost sight of the ground altogether. Suddenly the planet was rushing up to meet him and he landed with an undignified, one-legged, arm-swirling skid which ended when he pitched sideways into a clump of tobacco plants.

Winded and totally unnerved by his experience, he sat up and examined the red-and-gold boots with awe. The supply clerk at Fort Eccles had called them Startrooper Sevenleague boots, and Peace was belatedly realizing why – each had a miniature anti-gravity machine built into it. He was wondering if it would be safe to stand up again when a twig snapped some distance ahead of him. Peace looked up and saw a man in a tan uniform advancing cautiously through the haze. He was carrying an old type of firearm, which at once identified him as an Ulphan soldier, and he seemed almost as lost and bewildered as Peace felt.

Appalled and sickened by what he was doing, yet unable to disobey the command implanted in his mind, Peace raised his own vastly superior weapon. Anxious to give the Ulphan a quick, clean death, he aimed for the heart and pulled the trigger, unleashing a bolt of lethal radiation. A part of his mind was praying he would miss, but the deadly purple ray found its mark. The Ulphan clapped a hand to his chest, at the same time emitting a yelp of pain and surprise, then he spun round, levelled his rifle and squeezed off a burst of automatic fire in Peace's direction.

Unable to understand why his supposed dinosaur gun had been unable to knock over a medium-sized man, Peace hunkered down into cover. There was no time for speculation about what had gone wrong, because – obsolete or not – the Ulphan soldier's rifle was rapidly scything down his screen of vegetation, and it could only be a matter of seconds before a bullet ended Peace's brief career in the Legion. He decided, in desperation, that the Sevenleague boots which had got him into this predicament represented his only hope of escape.

Making himself ready for flight, he began wiggling his toes and felt the control buttons click downwards.

Peace snatched a deep breath as the antigrav units came into operation, but – in place of the dizzy ascent he had been expecting – the boots propelled him directly forward in a flat trajectory. The Ulphan's jaw sagged as he saw Peace, still in an undignified squatting position, zooming towards him through the murk. Dismayed by the further wayward behaviour of his footwear, Peace tried to stay on an even keel, but the boots surged ahead of his centre of gravity, tilting him backwards in the process. He felt a fierce impact on his behind and an instant later found himself seated squarely on the enemy soldier's chest. His red-and-gold boots were dislodged in the collision and, relieved of any load, soared off into the sky like frightened parakeets. He watched with mixed feelings as they disappeared towards the zenith, then became aware that he no longer had his rifle and was probably in mortal danger. He made a belated grab for his opponent's throat, but released it apologetically when he saw that the Ulphan, badly winded and unable to move, was gazing up at him in abject terror.

'Don't try anything,' Peace said, getting to his feet. He located the two fallen rifles and was picking them up when the figures of Dinkle, Ryan and Farr emerged from the surrounding smoke.

'Warren! How did you get ahead of us? I thought you were . . .' Ryan's eyes widened as he noticed the recumbent form of the Ulphan soldier. 'Is he dead?'

'No.' Peace looked curiously at the Ulphan's tan uniform and saw only a faint scorch mark on the left side of the chest. He turned to Dinkle and proffered his radiation rifle. 'Do you see anything wrong with this? I shot him from about twenty metres and all it did was make him mad.'

Dinkle shrugged. 'That always happens.'

'But we were told the rifles had unlimited range and . . .'

'Not in smoke – too much energy absorption by particles in the air. And it's the same in fog.' Dinkle savoured the morose pleasure that comes from imparting bad news. 'In fact, any time there's a touch of mist you could defend yourself better with a croquet mallet. And when there's smoke . . .'

'Correct me if I'm wrong,' Ryan put in, 'but aren't battlegrounds *usually* covered with smoke?'

'Only because the opposition generally uses obsolete equipment like guns and bombs and flame-throwers.'

'This is worse than I thought,' Ryan said, his plump face growing paler. 'Isn't anybody else equipped with radiation equipment?'

'Only our allies – the ones we've equipped with advanced arms.'

Dinkle glanced at his three companions to see if they appreciated the irony of his words, then went on to belabour the point. 'If we could just set up a system where we were friends with our enemies – and where we only fought our friends – we'd be all right. The trouble is . . .'

'I don't believe all this crap,' Farr said, giving a characteristic scowl. 'We beat Aspatria, didn't me? Cap'n Handy said it was a quick victory, too.'

Surprisingly, Dinkle showed signs of apprehension. 'If you ask me, it wasn't us or the Aspatrians who ended that war – it was the throwrugs. The throwrugs and the Oscars.'

The words had no sinister connotations that Peace knew of, yet he felt a flicker of unease. 'What are throwrugs and Oscars?'

'Be glad you don't know – I saw a throwrug get one of my buddies.' Dinkle's eyes seemed to lose focus, as though horrific memories were parading in front of him. 'Dropped out of a tree, it did. Straight on to him. Covered him up, just like a big rug, and started digesting him. I'll never forget those screams. It was a good thing for him I was right there. Lucky, he was.'

'You managed to pull it off him,' Ryan prompted.

Dinkle shook his head. 'I managed to shoot him before he'd suffered more'n a few seconds. Took a risk waiting around that long, but it was the least I could do for a pal.'

Ryan edged away from Dinkle. 'Don't do me any favours, will you? Any time you see me suffering just look the other . . .'

'What's going on here?' Lieutenant Merriman's voice was muffled by his gas mask as he came stumbling through the layered curtains of smoke. 'Why aren't you men moving up front?'

'Private Peace took a prisoner, sir.' Dinkle pointed at the recumbent Ulphan, who was showing the first signs of getting his breath back. 'We were just about to interrogate him.'

'Good work, Peace. Good thinking.' Merriman gave Peace an approving glance. 'I'll be sure to keep you up front in future.'

'Thank you, sir.' Peace was less than happy about this fresh development, but the combat incident just described by Dinkle had had a strangely disturbing effect on him, and the prospect of stopping an Ulphan bullet no longer seemed so terrible. His thoughts on the matter were interrupted by the discovery that his feet, unprotected by boots or shoes, seemed to have glued themselves to the ground. He looked down at them and saw he was standing in a patch of black goo which appeared to have seeped upwards through the soil. Holding his socks on with difficultly, he moved to a better position.

'I'll question the prisoner now.' Merriman nudged the Ulphan soldier with his toe. 'Listen to me, you cowardly extraterrestrial dog, you'd better tell me all you know about the strength and disposition of your forces in this area.'

The Ulphan raised himself on one elbow. 'Are you going to shoot me or torture me?'

'How dare you!' Merriman gave the others a scandalized glance. 'Terra doesn't treat her prisoners in that way.'

'In that case,' the Ulphan said comfortably, 'get lost.'

Merriman pulled his gas mask down in fury, received a lungful of the smoky atmosphere, and was forced to cover up again. He began choking and coughing, the rubberized mask clapping in and swelling horribly with each spasm, and what could be seen of his face turned a plummy crimson.

'You shouldn't have told him what you did, sir.' Dinkle pounded the lieutenant on the back. 'Let me try a different approach.'

'What can . . .?' Merriman wiped tears from his eyes. 'What can you do?'

'The old sympathetic bit, sir. It never fails. Just watch.' Dinkle took two flat packages from his pocket and knelt beside the prisoner. He opened one of the packages, exposing a row of slim white cylinders which appeared to be cigarettes, and held it out to the Ulphan. 'Have one of these.'

'Thanks.' The Ulphan took one of the cylinders, placed it between his lips and sucked eagerly. A contented expression spread over his face.

'What's going on?' Merriman demanded. 'That thing isn't even lit. What have you just given the prisoner?'

'The Ulphans use them instead of cigarettes, sir.' Dinkle stood up and showed the package to the officer. 'We captured a truck-load last week. The locals breathe tobacco smoke all the time, but they get a lift by sucking pure air through these long filters. This brand is just for hardened air-puffers, though – some of the Ulphans, specially the women, go in for these weaker ones.' He opened the second package and displayed a row of cylinders which looked like Earth-style filter cigarettes in reverse, each being mainly white filter with a short tobacco-packed section at one end.

'Disgusting habit,' Merriman said. 'See what you can get out of him.'

Dinkle returned to the prisoner and dropped the two packages into his hand. 'Have the lot, pal – compliments of the Legion.'

'Thanks.' The Ulphan slid open the flat trays and glanced inside. 'No coupons?'

Looking rather guilty, Dinkle handed over a bundle of blue chits. 'Now – how about some co-operation?'

The Ulphan inhaled deeply. 'Get lost.'

Peace, who felt a proprietory interest in the prisoner, started forward angrily to relieve him of the anti-smokes. The Ulphan promptly cowered away, his face distorted by fear.

'Don't let that one near me,' he babbled, his eyes pleading with Merriman. 'Don't let him jump on me.'

Merriman stared suspiciously at Peace. 'What did you do to this man?'

'I just . . . ah . . . jumped on him, sir. You know – unarmed combat.'

'I told you Warren was something special,' Ryan said to Copgrove Farr. 'I bet you Warren can get all the information we need.' He turned to Peace. 'Go ahead, Warren, let's see you jump on him.'

'I'll talk,' the Ulphan said, clutching at Merriman's leg. 'Look, I'm talking already. We haven't any men in this sector, apart from a few technicians and scouts. All the fire is coming from robot weapons, and if you detour round the back you can switch 'em all off.'

'No men?' Merriman said. 'Why's that?'

'It's that stuff.' The Ulphan pointed at the tacky patch in which Peace had been standing. 'This is a high tar area – most of our boys refuse to breathe the sort of smoke you get around here. Personally, I say it doesn't do you any harm. My grandfather breathed it every day and he lived to be ninety. What I say is, if you're . . .'

'Be quiet,' Merriman ordered. 'I'm not sure about this story of yours – it might be a cunning Ulphan trick. Robot weapons would be as big a danger to you as they would to us.'

The prisoner shook his head. 'We carry transmitters which broadcast a coded identity signal. You can have mine if you want – as long as I'm allowed to stay near it.'

'It definitely has gone quiet since he's been around,' Peace said. 'Not a shot or shell anywhere near us.'

'You've done well, Private Peace,' Merriman's thin voice was almost lost within his respirator, but his excitement was unmistakable. 'This could be a turning point in the battle, in the whole war. I'll report to Captain Handy immediately.' He raised his wrist communicator to the general region of his mouth. While he was talking to the captain, Ryan grasped Peace's hand and shook it energetically, and even Farr looked reluctantly amiable.

'Great stuff, Warren,' Ryan said. 'The way things were going here we wouldn't have lasted a week. Now it looks like victory celebrations all the way. I've always fancied riding into town on the side of a tank. Girls throwing flowers at me . . . girls throwing cigarettes at me . . . girls throwing *girls* at me . . .' He broke off, his attention caught by the slight but unmistakable argumentative tone which was creeping into Lieutenant Merriman's radio conversation. The note of dissension was all the more noticeable for being completely unexpected.

'With all due respect, sir,' Merriman was saying, 'I don't believe the Ulphans would feel any daunting psychological impact when they heard we had marched line abreast and unafraid against their robot guns. As a matter of fact, I think they would laugh their heads off. I realize how disappointed you must be at not getting another chance to prove your tactical theories, but . . .'

Merriman had to stop and listen for a moment, nodding his head. 'I didn't mean to imply that you were . . .'

He listened again, still nodding, and – incredibly – his shoulders began to droop. 'Yes, sir. I know it's a privilege to die for Terra.'

Ryan clutched Peace's arm. 'I don't like the sound of this, Warren.'

Lieutenant Merriman signed off and turned to face the others. He removed his gas mask, somehow managing not to cough, and his mouth travelled upwards and to the right on the fire curtain of teeth, assuming a comma-shape which was indicative of blighted illusion. Peace suddenly felt sorry for him.

'Captain Handy sends his congratulations,' the lieutenant said after a brief pause. 'You have proved yourselves such a valuable and resourceful combat team that you're to be trans-shipped immediately to the planet Threlkeld. You'll be there in a couple of hours. I'm going with you, of course.'

Ryan wiggled his fingers to attract the lieutenant's attention. 'Is Threlkeld an R&R world, sir?'

'Not unless you've got your own ideas about how to spell death and destruction – we're losing men there faster than we can ship them in.'

'Oh, God!' Ryan turned to Peace and his eyes hardened with accusation. 'This is your fault, Warren – we're on our way to a second war and we haven't even had a cup of coffee yet.'

Peace replied with the crudest swear word he could summon to mind, but he did it in an abstracted manner. It had become clear to him that he had only one chance of achieving a reasonable life span. No matter how impossible the task might appear, no matter how many difficulties lay in the way, he would have to regain his memory and thus invalidate his contract with the Legion. The problem was that there was simply nowhere for him to begin, and now that he was no longer on Earth the chances of finding someone who had known him in his previous existence seemed vanishingly small.

While he was trudging with the rest of the unit towards

the embarkation point. Peace's thoughts returned to the mystery surrounding his past. People kept assuring him that he must have been steeped in evil, but – on taking mental inventory – he was unable to find any antisocial urges within himself. This set him a philosophical poser – would he be able to recognize a criminal tendency if it was handed to him on a plate? Did any individual consciously think of himself as 'bad'? When even the most hardened wrongdoer was setting out to commit a misdeed, did he not feel as justified and as 'good' as any other member of society?

His speculations came to an end when the ship appeared, an angular dumb-bell which came down from the sky in a blurred arc and clumped into place on the soft ground. Its central doors sprang open without any visible human agency and Merriman gave the order for everybody to go on board. Peace trooped into the ship, wincing as his unshod feet encountered the chill of the metal floor, and dropped dejectedly onto a bench without taking part in the scramble for serviceable seat belts. The hazards of space flight were negligible compared to those of the battle zone and, being coldly realistic, he had less hope of escape than any other ranker in the entire Legion. Without a single clue to help him solve the mystery of his past, he was doomed to flit about the galaxy in ugly, identical-seeming ships and ...

Peace's eyes suddenly focused on a small blue object on the floor in front of him, and he realized the ship was actually the same one which had brought him to Ulpha. The last time he had seen the little plastic toad it had been squashed flat, but its molecular memory had enabled it to return to its original shape. Wishing he could be equally indestructible, Peace gathered up the little toad and gazed at it with something akin to affection – had it been able to speak it might have told him something about the person he used to be.

'What did you find? Dinkle, who had sat down near him unnoticed, leaned sideways for a better look. 'Huh! Somebody's been living it up.'

Peace gripped the toad just in time to prevent it springing away. 'What do you mean?'

'They give those things out at the Blue Toad on Aspatria.'

'The Blue Toad?' Peace felt a stirring of excitement. 'Is that a bar? Restaurant? Night Club?'

Dinkle nodded. 'The fanciest in Touchdown City. In fact, on the whole of Aspatria. It beats me why anybody would want to go to a place like that on a ranker's pay.'

'It all depends on how you look at things,' Peace said, dropping the toad safely into his pocket as he reached a secret decision. 'Some people can't stay away from places like that.'

chapter five

In some ways the yellow-skied planet of Threlkeld was less of a nightmare than Peace had expected.

The Ulphan campaign was a police action against dissident colonists – and Peace had been dismayed at the idea of humans fighting humans – but on Threlkeld the Legion was merely engaged in rendering a jungle continent safe for mining operations. Further easing his conscience was the fact that there was no intelligent species indigenous to the planet, the opposition to commercial development coming from an assortment of wild animals. And it was there that the list of good points about service life on Threlkeld came to an abrupt end.

The denizens of the Threlkeldian jungle were so ferocious, ugly and diverse as to create the impression that Nature had made the world a kind of sampler of animal nastiness. In her ingenuity she had produced beasts which trapped their prey by looking like plants, and carnivorous plants which trapped their prey by looking like animals. There were insects which actually thrived on being crushed underfoot, because their internal secretions could burn through a plastic sole in less than a second and also contained eggs which, on the instant of contacting flesh, produced hundreds of ravenous grubs which could reduce a human foot to a bootful of bones in less than a minute.

There were electric snakes, garrotte snakes and dagger snakes – all of which lived up to their names; grenade birds, tomahawk birds and skullpeckers – all of which lived up to their names; and armoured monsters so tenacious of life that even when they were sliced up by rayitzers their individual limbs leaped about like giant demented jackboots for as long as half a day, often enabling the parent to commit more mayhem in kit form than it had been capable of as a single entity.

Every man in the 203rd had his own particular bête noire, and there were lots of those around as well. Peace's greatest dislike was reserved for the multichew, a composite beast which at first glance looked like a huge caterpillar, but whose segments were animals in their own right. Each module was roughly cheese shaped, with four powerful stubby legs, a vicious set of jaws, and neural interfaces on the upper and lower surfaces. Segments were dangerous enough as individuals – scuttling, malevolent footstools which were difficult to hit with rifle fire – but when ten or twelve of them formed a chain and became a full-blown multichew, their fearsomeness was increased in proportion. Peace had found it necessary to destroy at least half of the composite animal to bring it down, whereupon the undamaged segments would promptly separate and renew the attack from all sides. It was at this stage he felt a belated gratitude towards Savoury Shrimp Sauce Inc for spending its meagre funds on protective cups rather than on more decorative but less functional items of apparel.

He also felt a renewed determination to proceed with his escape plan, such as it was.

The first step was to prise a vital scrap of information out of Lieutenant Merriman, but securing an interview with him proved difficult because the lieutenant, apparently having recovered all his patriotic fervour, spent most of his waking hours where the fighting was at its height. It was not until the third day on Threlkeld that Peace managed to corner him near the field kitchen, and Merriman's mouth made several unsuccessful attempts to compress with displeasure when he realized he was trapped.

'I can't talk to you now, Peace,' he said in a piping voice, moving away. 'We can't serve Terra by standing around jawing.'

'But that's just it, sir,' Peace countered, uttering the only words he could think of which would grip the young officer's interest, 'I believe we could.'

Merriman turned back. 'What's on your mind, Peace?'

'Well, sir, we've been losing a lot of men to the multichews, and . . . and . . .' Peace listened, aghast, as his own mouth uttered the lie. 'I've thought of a better way to fight them.'

'I'm listening.'

'Well . . .' Peace's mind raced as he sought inspiration. 'Well, they're most dangerous when a dozen or so of them join up together, and all we've got to do is prevent that happening.'

'How?'

'Spray them with oil, sir. So that they keep slipping off each other. Any sort of lubricant would do – even suntan oil.'

'That,' Merriman said ominously, 'is a rotten idea.'

Peace, who had formed exactly the same opinion, caught his arm. 'Or we could spray them with something to block the nerve signals between the different segments. Any quick-drying varnish would do. How about hair lacquer?'

'What would the people back on Terra think of the Legion if we started requisitioning suntan lotion and hair sprays?' Merriman detached his arm from Peace's grip and stared at him suspiciously. 'Is this some kind of subversive greeno trick?'

'Please don't say things like that, sir,' Peace said earnestly, at last feeling the conversation veer in the direction he wanted. 'Nobody could be more loyal to the Legion and to you. I'd like you to know it isn't the command enforcer that makes me obey your orders – it's my love of . . . er . . . Terra, and my respect for you as an officer.'

'Don't try to cream me.'

'It's the truth, sir.'

'If I thought you really meant that . . .'

'I do, sir, I do.'

'Why, thank you, Peace. This is the very first time that anybody has . . .' Merriman blinked several times, then took out a handkerchief and blew his nose. 'I sometimes wish that more of the Supreme Command had been like General Nightingale and held out against command enforcers in their own divisions. I mean, how am I ever going to *know* if I've got inborn leadership or not?'

'It's a terrible problem, sir – and all because somebody put a stupid little diaphragm into your throat, vibrating away at . . . what sort of frequency would you say? Eight or ten thou per second?'

'Twelve,' Merriman said abstractedly. 'You know, Peace, I've enjoyed this little talk with you. I had no idea you were so sensitive and . . . Where are you going, Peace?'

'I'm needed at the front, sir.' Peace gestured towards the wall of viridescent jungle which represented the limit of human-controlled territory. Needles of light from radiation rifles burned irregularly in the shade of the overhanging vegetation, and occasional purple flashes showed that rayitzers were in action. The air was filled with the shouts of men and the roars, honks and hisses of the various fauna which were slowly being displaced from their native territories. As he ran towards the firing line Peace felt a certain amount of guilt about his psychological manipulation of the lieutenant, but if he was to stay alive he could not afford to be scrupulous about his methods.

He scanned the surroundings carefully and within a matter of seconds had located his next major requirement – a supply of electronics components. It took the form of a radiation rifle, lying in the undergrowth, which had been grotesquely distorted by some act of violence. Peace had little doubt that its former owner was in a similar condition, and therefore he was relieved to find there were no organic residues to be wiped off the weapon before he could make use of it. He picked up the rifle, snapped out the ray generator pack and dropped it into his pocket.

At that moment an adult whippersnapper, busily performing both the actions for which it was named, leaped at him from the lower branches of a tree and he spent the next minute beating it off with the broken weapon while his own rifle hung uselessly on his back. He was sweating profusely and gibbering with panic by the time he managed to stun the beast and dispatch it with a five-second squirt of radiation.

The incident was a sharp reminder of what would inevitably happen if he did not remain fully alert. He decided to put all thoughts of the escape plan out of his head until conditions were more suitable for cerebration. A second reminder came an hour later when, only a few metres away, the volatile Latin recruit, whose name Peace had never learned, was scooped up by a scaly monster and – yodelling a final, despairing 'Mamma mia!' – was stuffed into its cavernous maw.

When darkness had put an end to the day's fighting the remnants of Lieutenant Merriman's unit were sent back to the shelter of an encampment, given a bowl of gruel each and allowed to rest on heaps of dried grass. Tired though the recruits were, most were unable to sleep because the grass had been gathered locally and had a disturbing habit of moving about of its own accord and trying to take root in any bodily orifices it could reach.

Peace settled down in a corner and, pausing only to break off exploring tendrils of straw, began dismantling the rifle generator pack. The light in the tent was rather dim for intricate work, but he was pleased to discover that his fingers had an in-built gift for dealing with the circuitry. It would have meant the end of his scheme if the knowledge of electronics he had divined within himself had been as far out of touch with reality as his ideas about spaceships.

He worked for two hours, grateful for the extensive use of button terminals which enabled him to rebuild circuits without soldering equipment, and at the end of that time had created a small device which would, within a limited radius, neutralize all sound vibrations in the frequency range upon which the Legion's command enforcers operated. It took him a further ten minutes to fit the gadget into his helmet, then he lay down to sleep, well satisfied with his progress.

Ryan, who had been watching with covert interest, raised himself on one elbow. 'Hey, Warren – what's that thing you just put in your helmet?'

'Keep your voice down,' Peace whispered. 'I don't want everybody to know about it.'

'But what is it?'

'It's . . . ah . . . a miniature hi-fi.' Peace conducted an imaginary orchestra for a few seconds. 'When I go, I want to go with music in my ears.'

'I wish I could build something like that,' Ryan said admiringly. 'All I know about hi-fi is that there's a main speaker and a tweeter, and some circuits in between to make sure that . . .'

'Never the main shall tweet,' Peace cut in. 'That's an ancient joke, Vernie, and it was rotten even when it was first invented. Do you mind if we get some sleep?'

'Only trying to cheer us up, Warren. Don't you like gags?'

'If I had a gag right now I'd roll it up tight and . . .' Peace fell into an exhausted sleep before he could finish the sentence, and for the remainder of that night he dreamed the short, simplistic dreams appropriate to a man whose personal memory went back only three days.

Being deaf to the special harmonics in officers' voices gave Peace a considerable degree of freedom. He had to make a show of promptly obeying every direct order, but as soon as he was out of sight of the officer concerned he could – in the confusion of the battle zone – safely return to his own pursuits. The command enforcer system positively aided him in this because the idealistic young lieutenants who made up the command cadre never thought of querying his activities as long as he went about them with a suffi- ciently grim and purposeful look.

On his first day of comparative liberty he went to the flattened area used for spaceship landings and was disap- pointed to find that his new ideas about the vessels were wrong in one important respect. Having rid himself of the concept of spaceships looking like graceful gleaming spires, he had formed the notion that at each end of the rectangular structures there were hand-operated roller signs announcing their destinations. When he saw, instead, the featureless metal walls of the transceiver towers he had to accept that his visualized signs belonged to some other mode of transportation, and this led to a new thought.

He had proved that he still retained an excellent knowledge of electronics, and yet the machine used on him at Fort Eccles – designed to wipe out all memories associated with his guilt and remorse – had chosen to obliterate everything he must have known about spaceship technology and operation. Did this mean that his life had been intimately concerned with spacecraft? Had he been a pilot? Or a spaceship designer?

Peace toyed with the idea that he might be able to identify his previous areas of expertise by listing all the subjects of which he currently knew nothing; then came the realization that it was difficult to discriminate between natural and induced ignorance. Did the fact that he knew nothing whatsoever about the breeding habits of *Anobium punctatum* prove that he had been a woodworm eradicator?

Deciding that action was better than introspection, he returned his attention to the present. He had set his heart on reaching the planet Aspatria, and to that end began spending as much time as possible around the landing area, hoping to stow himself away on a ship going in the right direction. His first plan was to question crew members about their destinations, but dozens of ship arrivals and take-offs went by without his seeing a single astronaut and he developed a strong suspicion that the vessels were fully automatic in their operation. He then took to questioning departing rankers about their destinations. This activity, apart from bringing him close to being apprehended by an unusually alert officer, produced only the information that – incredible though it might seem – there were other war zones which made Threlkeld look like a picnic ground.

Three days after he had built his command neutralizer, Peace and his unit were shipped out to Torver, a rainy world where the morose Copgrove Farr died horribly as a result of kicking a toadstool which exploded with such violence that millions of its spores passed through his clothing and skin. By the time his fellow legionaries buried him, ten minutes later, he was sprouting fungi from head to foot. Peace awarded Farr a posthumous forgiveness for various remarks made about the thinness of his legs. He also redoubled his efforts to find a ship heading for Aspatria.

A week later Lieutenant Merriman and his unit were moved on to the planet Hardknott, where the unlucky Private Benger swarmed up a tree to escape from a pack of armourdillos and was promptly devoured by the tree itself. By this time Peace was becoming desperate, even though he inherited Benger's shoes, which proved a remarkably good fit once he had shaken out of them all that remained of their donor. When he turned in at night he would speculate, in the few seconds before sleep claimed him, on why the crooked lawyers who drew up the Legion's service contract had taken such pains to secure his labour for thirty, forty or fifty years. The way things were going with the 203rd, it was a statistical certainty that – even with his invention enabling him to disobey the more suicidal orders – he would be poisoned, crushed, torn apart or eaten within a matter of weeks. There was even a possibility of his meeting all of those fates at more or less the same time.

*

Like the other men in his unit, Peace found himself crying quite a lot, and becoming thinner and more jumpy with every passing day. By the end of the first month Vernie Ryan's plumpness had disappeared and the shreds of his green glitter suit hanging around him created the impression he was covered with some form of seaweed. Private Dinkle, who had had more combat time than either of them, developed a nervous tic and a habit of crossing himself and muttering gloomily about Armageddon.

'The way he talks about Armageddon,' Ryan whispered to Peace over his breakfast gruel one morning, 'you'd think it was the end of the world.'

'I warned you about those blasted jokes,' Peace replied, grabbing a convenient strip of Ryan's suit and twisting it round his neck. He began to apply pressure, then realized the enormity of what he was doing and relaxed his grip. 'I'm sorry, Vernie. I think I'm cracking up.'

'It's all right,' Ryan said, massaging his throat. 'I used to be a professional comic, you know, and my gags used to have the same effect on people even when times were good.'

'I can't remember any good times – that's the trouble. As far as I'm concerned, it's always been like this.' Peace felt in his pocket for his blue toad, the small companion which had once offered him a crumb of hope. 'But that's no excuse for getting rough with you.'

'Let's forget it.'

Peace nodded miserably. He stroked the smooth plastic of the toad with his thumb, wishing it could summon a genie with the power to grant his dearest wishes.

The entrance flap of the mess tent was lifted up and Lieutenant Merriman came through the triangular opening. Something about his appearance struck Peace as being highly unusual; then he realized that the lieutenant had left off his battle dress and was spruced up in a smart new uniform. He was accompanied by a timid-looking sergeant who had a box filled with small buff envelopes. The sergeant was also carrying an armful of flimsy blue clothing.

'Gather round,' Merriman cried. 'This is it! The day you've all been waiting for!'

'What day is that, sir?' Ryan said cautiously.

'Leave day, of course. Didn't I tell you?'

'No, sir.' Ryan gave the others a glance of round-eyed surmise. 'Do we get time off?'

'What a question!' Merriman's mouth tried to stretch itself into a grin, but as this set up an impossible stress on the limited amount of lip material available it had to content itself with several rapid oscillations at the corners. 'What a silly question! Did you really think your commanding officers were too lofty and too remote to appreciate how much strain you've been under? No, men, we know only too well that you can't fight off battle fatigue indefinitely, that you need time in which to relax, to recuperate, to let the mental scars heal themselves.'

'That's great, sir. How much time do we get?'

Merriman glanced at his watch. 'Well, Ryan, as you've been in the Legion for thirty days, you're entitled to three hours.'

Ryan stepped back. 'I'll be buggered!'

'Language!' Merriman said, frowning, then his brow cleared. 'Don't worry, Ryan – it's within my discretion to allow you and Peace some extra rest and recreation time as a reward for loyal service, and that's what I'm going to do. You're going to enjoy the maximum leave period with the rest of the unit. Four hours.'

'*Four hours*,' Ryan whispered. 'I don't believe this. It's too much.'

'No – you've earned it, and you'll be even more pleased to hear that it doesn't include travelling time.' Merriman swelled with benevolence as he beamed at Ryan. 'Your four hours won't even *begin* until you step off the ship on Aspatria.'

Peace, who had been listening to the conversation with considerable interest, felt his heart give a wild lurch at the mention of Aspatria. He resolved to do nothing which might attract undue attention and, simultaneously, his fingers opened of their own accord and allowed his bowl of gruel to upend itself in his lap. Lieutenant Merriman stared at him with distaste as he got to his feet and tried to brush the porridge off his ragged hose.

'What are you getting so excited about, Peace?' Merriman said. 'You aren't hoping to desert on Aspatria, are you?'

'Of course not, sir.' Peace simpered at him in a manner he hoped would be expressive of total loyalty and devotion to duty.

'That's good, because . . .' Merriman fingered the lump on his throat, '. . . I'm giving you all a direct order to be back at the Legion field and on board ship – ready to leave – not more than four hours after we reach Touchdown City. Now, line up and collect your pay packets and leave suits.'

Peace queued with the rest of the unit and was issued with an envelope bearing his name, together with a two-piece suit of a material which resembled crepe paper. He was grateful for the Legion's consideration in providing clean clothing until he opened his packet and found that, of the three hundred monits due to him, a hundred had been deducted for the paper suit and a further forty had been put into the regiment's retirement fund. The latter item, considering the average life expectancy of a legionary, suggested corruption in high places, but at least he still had the price of a good meal in the Blue Toad.

And, with luck, during the two hours or so that it would take to consume it he would pick up a vital clue to his past.

He had no clear idea of what he was hoping to find – perhaps a waiter who remembered him, perhaps his name and address on a creditputer card – but this was the only chance he had and he was determined to grasp it with both hands. It would be necessary for him to hide out when his desertion was noticed by the Legion, but in its three centuries of existence Touchdown City had grown large enough to house a population of four million, and he was confident he could remain undiscovered for weeks or months. That, hopefully, would be ample time in which to follow up any clues he found. There was always the possibility that he had never actually been near Aspatria, that he had found or been given the little plastic souvenir, but this did not bear contemplation and he pushed the idea out of his mind.

Lieutenant Merriman led his depleted band to a waiting ship, which proved different from the type Peace already knew in that the passenger compartment was larger and included a locker room with toilet and shower facilities. As soon as the klaxon had sounded, and the vessel had begun its inertialess flight, he went into the locker room where the sergeant, who also served as toilet attendant, gave him the option of a cold shower for five monits or a hot one for twenty. Peace chose the expensive luxury, but economized by not renting a shaver to remove the short red-gold beard he had grown during his month of service. The face which gazed back at him in the mirror was leaner, harder and more mature than the one he remembered.

'What do you think of the beard?' he said to Ryan, who was donning his paper suit close by.

'It gives you a certain *je ne sais quoi*,' Ryan replied, 'but I don't know what it is.'

Peace stared at his companion. 'Another of your so-called jokes?'

'What do you mean so-called?' Ryan said indignantly.

77

'You're lucky to have me around to cheer you up.'

'Perhaps you're right.' It dawned on Peace that he had developed a real affection for Ryan, the only friend he could remember having, and that if his plans worked out they would shortly be parting for ever. It was ironic that he, who had begun by earnestly committing his life to the Legion, was about to make an early escape, while Ryan – who had joined in the spirit of somebody taking a week at a health farm – was doomed to soldier on until he died. Peace thought about the matter for a few seconds and decided to take a dangerous risk. He glanced around the room to make sure nobody could see what he was doing, then he took Ryan's plastic helmet out of his locker and replaced it with his own.

Ryan looked perplexed. 'What's the idea, Warren?'

'I'm giving you my built-in hi-fi.' Peace pointed at the command neutralizer before concealing it by turning the helmet over. 'I won't need it any more.'

'But what about when you come back?' Ryan's voice faded as he saw that Peace was shaking his head. 'Warren, are you saying what I think you're saying? I knew you were a bright boy, but this is too . . .'

Peace signalled him to keep quiet and in a confidential whisper explained how his invention operated. 'It'll help you to stay alive till you get a good chance to duck out,' he concluded. 'Do it in a battle zone, if possible, and they'll write you off as missing, presumed dead. They won't even bother to look for you.'

'Why aren't you doing that?'

'I've got business on Aspatria,' Peace said. 'At least, I think I have. Perhaps I'll see you around.'

'I hope so. And I hope you find what you're looking for, Warren.'

The two men shook hands and, feeling quite distressed, Peace hurried out into the passenger compartment and dropped on to a bench beside Private Dinkle, who was staring dully at the floor. At the impact of Peace's arrival, Dinkle started violently, crossed himself and sank back into his gloomy torpor.

'Cheer up, Bud,' Peace said. 'You're going on *leave*!'

Dinkle stirred slightly. 'On Aspatria? You can keep it.'

'Bad scene, is it?'

'Not any more, it isn't – not since we beat hell out of the Aspatrians back in '83.'

'But you're not happy about going there?'

Dinkle nodded slowly. 'Too many memories.'

'My trouble is I haven't enough.'

'You wouldn't say that if you'd ever had to shoot a buddy who had a throwrug over him. There oughta be a limit to what a man has to do.'

Peace felt an inexplicable chill. His brief spell in the Legion had made him conversant with many unpleasant ways of entering the hereafter, but the scene described by Dinkle always had the effect of making his blood corpuscles turn into millions of tiny clunking ice cubes. He shivered slightly and tried to offer a little comfort.

'What's done,' he said, 'is done.'

Dinkle fixed him with a leaden eye. 'Is that some advanced philosophy? Have you just extended the boundaries of human thought?'

'There's no need to take it like that,' Peace said, offended. 'All I meant was . . . the past's over and done with.'

'The Oscar's aren't over and done with, sonny.' Dinkle crossed himself once more.

The strange dread returned to Peace in full force, but his curiosity was aroused. 'What are these Oscars you keep talking about?'

'Supermen, sonny. Big guys with bald heads and muscles all over the place. They look like they're made out of polished bronze.'

'They sound like statues.'

'Statues can't move.' Dinkle's voice took on a hollow quality. 'But Oscars can run like the wind, and they can smash down trees with their bare hands, and nothing hurts them. Radiation, bullets, bombs – everything just bounces off. They're really what ended the war on Aspatria. Even the officers got to be afraid of them, so they pulled us out of all the up-country forests.'

'I don't get this,' Peace said. 'Are the Oscars the native Aspatrians?'

'You college types don't know much about the real galaxy, do you?' Dinkle stopped brooding on the past long enough to give Peace a look of contempt. 'Aspatria is a human colony – one of the oldest there is. In fact, that's what the war was about. Just because they'd been around for three centuries or so, and were a few thousand light years from Earth, they thought they could go independent and stop paying their taxes. What would happen to the Federation if every Tom, Dick and Harry decided . . .?'

'But who are the Oscars?' Peace cut in. 'Where did they come from?'

'Nobody knows officially. They appeared back on Aspatria back around '82 or '83. Some people say they're mutants, but I know better.' Dinkle's face began to twitch and his voice grew louder. 'Soldiers of the Devil – that's what they are – mustering for the last big battle between good and evil. And they're going to win! I tell you, Warren, Armageddon's almost on us, and we're on the losing side.'

'Calm down,' Peace said uneasily as men in other parts of the room began to glance in Dinkle's direction. He had wanted to remain as unobtrusive as possible before quietly slipping away, but Dinkle's story had a hypnotic fascination for him. 'What makes you so sure the Oscars are evil?'

'I've seen them in action.' Dinkle crossed himself again and his eyes glazed over. 'Got separated from my unit one day . . . making my own way back through the forest when I heard this noise . . . got down on my hands and knees and crawled up to the edge of a clearing for a look-see . . . and I saw . . . I saw about five Oscars there . . . and they had some of our boys with them, lying there on the ground . . .

'Our boys were wounded, you see. I could hear them moaning and groaning and pleading for mercy, but it was no use. The Oscars kept right on doing it . . .' Dinkle covered his face with his hands. 'I can't go on.'

'You've got to.' An icy breeze seemed to be stirring the hair on the nape of Peace's neck, but his mind was totally in thrall to the ghastly story Dinkle was unfolding. 'What were the Oscars doing?'

'They were feeding our boys to the . . . *to the throw-rugs.*'

Peace felt his stomach heave. 'Oh, my God! You don't mean . . .'

'It's true, Warren. The Oscars had collected up some throwrugs – they could do that, you see, because nothing hurts them – and they were throwing them over our boys while they lay there on the ground. I can still hear them screaming and pleading for quick deaths. I can still see them writhing around while the throwrugs digested them and . . .' Dinkle clawed his fingers into Peace's knee. 'Know something else, Warren?'

'What?'

'The Oscars were *laughing.* They enjoyed seeing good men being eaten alive. If I'd been a brave man I'd have gone in there with my rifle and tried to put our boys out of their misery – but I was a coward, Warren. I was too scared of the same thing being done to me – so I crawled away and saved my own skin. I don't deserve to be alive.'

The blood was pounding in Peace's ears as he stood up. 'Listen, Bud,' he said, seeking a way to change the subject, 'why don't you clean up and change into your leave suit? It'll make you feel better.'

Dinkle shook his head. 'I don't need any leave suit. I'm staying right here in the ship till we take off again.'

'Why's that?'

Dinkle hunched around the slim prop of his rifle. 'I'm not going to risk bumping into no Oscars. They swagger around like they own the place, and everybody's afraid of them. I've heard they can read people's minds, and if I saw them that day . . .' Dinkle crossed himself several times in quick succession and began swaying and muttering wildly about Armageddon, retribution and the Day of Judgment.

Peace backed away from him in consternation and took refuge in the lee of the coffee machine until, some minutes later, the klaxon sounded to announce that the ship was going into the landing phase. As soon as the floor had given its familiar conclusive lurch he joined the group of men clustered around the exit. After a tantalizing pause the door slid open and revealed an expanse of sunlit grass which could have been a pasture instead of a landing field. The air was warm and sweet and in the distance, shining with harmonious pastels, was the graceful architecture of the city.

Peace felt an immediate liking for what he could see of Aspatria and he wondered if that could be a sign of previous acquaintance with the place. He stepped out with the others on to the pliant turf, filling his lungs with the scented air, revelling in the freedom from physical danger, then became aware of a different kind of hazard. Lieutenant Merriman had decided to address his men, yet again, on the evils of tobacco and alcohol, and – as he had a tendency to repeat everything he said – was almost certain to reiterate his order about returning to the ship within four hours. Peace was now unprotected by the command neutralizer and if he heard the order he would have no choice but to obey.

'Over there you will find a spaceport coach which will take you into Touchdown City,' Merriman said, pointing towards a complex of low buildings. 'Visit as many museums and art galleries as you possibly can, but don't forget that you . . .'

Whimpering with alarm, Peace clapped his hands over his ears, doubled low and scuttled away along the side of the spaceship. On rounding the corner of the transceiver tower he glanced back and, although it was difficult to be certain, got the impression that some of the blue-suited figures had turned to watch his departure – which must have looked slightly odd, not to say suspicious. Cursing himself for having blundered at such an early stage in his scheme, he looked around for an escape route and saw that the field's perimeter was within sprinting distance. He ran towards it, expecting at any moment to hear a hue and cry developing in his wake, and reached the five-strand wire fence. Praying the wires were not electrified, he clambered through into the longer grass beyond. Ahead of him was a gentle rise which he ascended at top speed. On the crest he looked back and was relieved to see that neither Lieutenant Merriman nor any of his former comrades had emerged into view behind the rectangular hulk of the ship.

Relaxing a little, Peace took stock of his surroundings. The land fell away before him in a long and rather steep grassy bank, at the bottom of which a substantial road curved off in the direction of the city. A limousine painted in the unmistakable brash yellow of a taxi was cruising along the road. Peace considered using it as a quick and providential means of getting into the city, then decided against it on the grounds that he would need to conserve what was left of his money. He set off at an angle down the slope, determined to move at a leisurely pace and regain his composure. The lushness of the grass made the going slippery, and almost at once his thighs began to quiver with the effort of holding himself back on the incline. He began walking faster and faster, losing more control with each second, and before he really knew what was happening he was bounding down the long bank at breakneck speed.

I'll learn from this little experience, he thought, trying to preserve a detached calm while the wind whistled in his ears and his contacts with the ground grew more fleeting. *One should always expect the unexpected.*

At that moment, as if to ratify his conclusions, the unexpected occurred again. On the road below, the driver of the cruising taxi – apparently under the impression that the flailing of Peace's arms was intended to draw his attention – flashed his headlights and brought his vehicle to a halt at a point where he judged Peace's descent would terminate. He must have had a keen eye for angles and distances, because Peace found himself hurtling straight at the taxi with no way of stopping, or even slowing down.

'Oh, no' he shouted. 'Out of the way, you fool!' The image of the taxi ballooned in his vision with frightening rapidity.

The driver looked out of his side window, making ready to welcome his fare, and his jaw sagged as he belatedly realized his peril. He was still struggling with the handbrake when Peace ran into the taxi with outstretched hands and beat the side window in on top of him.

Peace, whose chin had collided painfully with the vehicle's roof, fell back onto the grass.

'You maniac!' the taxi driver shouted, brushing glass

confetti out of his hair and off his shoulders with trembling hands. 'What did you want to do that for?'

'What did I . . .?' Peace gaped at him. 'What did you want to stop there for?'

'You hailed me . . . and, besides, I can stop anywhere I want.'

'I didn't hail you, and I can walk anywhere *I* want.'

'Call that walking?' The driver sneered through the newly formed aperture in the side of his car. 'You Blue-asses from Earth are all the same. Still sore about '83, so when you come here on leave you get all tanked up and start throwing your weight around. Well let me tell you, Mister Blue-ass – this is going to cost you.'

'Why should we be sore about . . .? What do you mean, it's going to cost me?'

'A hundred monits for a new window, and twenty for my loss of time.'

It was Peace's turn to sneer. 'You can whistle for it.'

'Suits me.' The driver raised a large, complex-looking whistle which had been hanging on a cord around his neck. 'I like using these subetheric jobs. You never know who's going to answer the call first – the police or the Oscars.' He put the instrument to his lips.

'I'll pay,' Peace said hastily, getting to his feet and producing his emaciated roll of bills. He counted off the required amount and passed it over.

'That's better,' the driver grumbled. 'I don't know what's the matter with folks these days – hailing cabs and then claiming they didn't. It must be a new craze.'

'Look, I'm sorry about damaging your taxi,' Peace said. 'How about taking me into the city?'

'Ten monits – and that's half price.'

'Okay.' Peace was concerned about his reserves of cash, now approaching zero, but it had occurred to him that the taxi driver could be a good source of information about day-to-day life on Aspatria. He got into the vacant front seat, noticing as he did so that a small rent had already appeared in the sleeve of his new suit. The car surged forward with a low whine from its unimagnetic engine and the brilliant yellow-green landscape became a flowing panoramic lightshow.

'Nice day,' the driver said, seemingly ready to forgive and forget. He was a long-faced man with watered-down hair. 'Nice place for a furlough.'

'Very nice.' Peace gave the scenery an approving nod. 'I don't know anything about Touchdown City and I . . .'

'Don't worry – I'll take you to the right place.'

'You will?'

'Sure. There's nothing in it for me, of course – no commission or anything like that – but make sure Big Nelly writes my name in the book as you go in. Trev, they call me. Don't forget – Trev.'

'You've got the wrong idea, Trev.' Peace tried not to show his indignation. 'I want to go to the Blue Toad.'

'You can't afford it, soldier.' Trev gave Peace an amiable double nudge with his elbow. 'Listen, you're bound to be starving – all the legionaries I pick up are starving – and I bet you like good music, too.'

'Good music?' Peace felt he was losing the thread of the conversation.

'Sure. My cousin runs this place called the Handel Bar. High class it is – because everything's named after highbrow composers and such – but it's cheap. There's nothing in it for me, of course – no commission or anything like that – but for twenty monits you'd get a big plate of his speciality, Chopin's Bolognaise, with loads of sonata ketchup, or a Minuet Steak, or a . . .'

'It sounds like a wonderful place,' Peace said, 'but I have to go to the Blue Toad.'

'Suit yourself – it's not as if there was anything in it for me – or if you just want a quick snack there's the Strauss Malts or . . .'

'Tell me about the Oscars,' Peace interrupted, returning to a subject which had a baleful fascination for him. 'Did you say they'd answer if you blew that police whistle?'

'Sometimes they do.' Trev remained quiet for a moment, showing he had been hurt by the rejection of his commercial advances. 'Sometimes they don't.'

'But why do they do it at all?'

'Nobody knows. They never talk to anybody, but there are some things they don't like – specially violent crime – and, boy, if you ever do anything an Oscar doesn't like you're in big trouble.'

'Are they like vigilantes?'

'Except you could get away from a vigilante – you can't get away from an Oscar.'

Peace turned the new information over in his mind, trying to reconcile the notion of enigmatic, superhuman crime-busters with the atrocity scene described by Bud Dinkle. 'Is it true they can read minds?'

'Some people say they can.' Trev gave Peace a thoughtful glance. 'What's it to you, anyway? You some kind of crook or something?'

'Of course not,' Peace replied. He lapsed into a broody silence while he reviewed his misfortunes. Not only had he been deprived of all memory and identity, not only was he alone on an alien planet, not only was he almost penniless and with no place to sleep, not only was he a deserter who would soon be pursued by the Space Legion – it could easily turn out that he had a criminal record on Aspatria. And if that were the case he was likely to be hounded down and punished by invincible, telepathic supermen whose idea of light relaxation was feeding wounded Earthmen to monsters.

'Cheer up,' Trev said as the taxi swung into a wide

boulevard which ran through the centre of Touchdown City. 'There's always somebody worse off than yourself.'

This was a thesis which Peace would have liked to dispute, but almost at once he saw – standing out with a vivid clarity from the other business signs – a tridi light sculpture in the shape of an enormous blue toad. He stared at it unblinkingly until the taxi came to a halt outside the building, where it floated like an insubstantial balloon. It was possible that his moment of truth was at hand, and – if so – it had found him in a condition in which he would have preferred several decades of reassuring lies.

He paid off the taxi and, realizing the necessity to act quickly before his nerve failed, squared his shoulders and walked in through the expensive, smooth-gliding doors of the Blue Toad.

chapter six

The foyer in which Peace found himself standing featured textile carpets and antique tubular chrome furniture, and he knew at once that all the warnings he had received had been justified. Even the air in the Blue Toad had an expensive smell to it. He began to doubt if the ten monits remaining in his pocket would buy anything more than a cup of coffee, which meant that his time in the place would be sharply limited unless he thought of a way of stalling.

'Was there something sir wanted?' The head waiter who had appeared from behind an ornamental grille was dressed in the full old-world regalia of denims and polo-neck sweater. He had pale blue eyes which stared coldly from the centre of a pink and puffy face, making it clear that he had no misconceptions about Peace's social or financial status. Peace instinctively covered the rip in the sleeve of his paper suit, then realized he was – as the *maître de* had intended – getting off on the wrong psychological footing. A man, he decided, who had successfully fought off a pack of enraged multichews had no business letting himself be cowed by an elderly waiter, no matter how splendidly attired that waiter might be.

The head waiter cleared his throat. 'Was there something that sir wanted?'

Peace donned a look of mingled surprise and irritation. 'Food, of course. You don't get many people coming in here to buy surgical trusses, do you?' He glanced around with a critical eye. 'Or have I come to the wrong place?'

The waiter's face stiffened. 'The main dining room is on your left, sir.'

'I know that.' Peace took the plastic blue toad from his pocket and flicked it in the air. 'Don't you remember me?'

The head waiter examined Peace's face. 'No, sir,' he said, looking somewhat relieved. 'Should I?'

'Never mind.' Hiding his disappointment, Peace walked towards the restaurant. 'Table for one – near the windows.'

A floor waiter, a younger man who was also wearing formal denims, showed him to a seat and provided him with a menu.

'I don't think we need bother with the menu,' Peace said, giving the waiter a democratic nudge. 'Just bring me my usual.'

The waiter blinked several times. 'Your usual what, sir?'

'*You* know.' Peace nudged him again, more forcibly. 'My usual – what I always have when I come here.'

The waiter moved out of range of Peace's elbow. 'I know all my regulars, and sir isn't one of them. If sir would like to consult the menu I'm sure . . .'

'I don't want to consult the menu,' Peace whispered fiercely. 'Look, there must be somebody out in the kitchen who knows me. Tell them I want my usual.'

The waiter gazed at Peace in perplexity for a moment, then comprehension dawned in his eyes. 'I'm with sir, now,' he said.

'Good! I'm glad about that.' Peace stared hopefully at him, wondering exactly what he had achieved.

'Sir can rely on me, of course.' The waiter leaned close to Peace, opened the menu and lowered his voice to an oily conspiratorial murmur. 'There's no disgrace in not being able to read – many quite intelligent people suffer from word-blindness – but if sir will pretend to study the menu I'll tell sir what each item means, and that way . . .'

'I can read it myself, you fool.' Peace snatched the heavy booklet away from him, temporarily abandoning his quest, and scanned the printed pages. His heart sank as he saw that the tariff, instead of being quoted in the common contraction of monits, was given in monetary units – the sort of traditional touch usually associated with exorbitant prices. His worst fears were confirmed when he looked at the figures themselves and found that coffee was thirty monits a cup, with a minimum cover charge of a hundred. He broke into a gentle sweat. All his hopes for the future, and for his past, were based on spending as long a time as possible in the restaurant and being seen by the maximum number of regular customers and staff. This meant that, regardless of ethics, he would have to order a sizeable meal in the full knowledge that he was unable to pay for it, and not think about the consequences until they came. The decision, though not an easy one, was influenced by the fierce gnawing in his stomach, which for a full month had known nothing but gruel and leathery strips of jerky.

Taking a deep breath, Peace ordered one of the most expensive meals possible – a seven-course affair centred around a speciality dish of Aspatrian lobster cooked in imported champagne. He eagerly swallowed three aperitifs and had downed most of a generous serving of soup when he remembered that his main objective was to prolong his stay in the establishment and be on the alert for contacts. Slowing his spoon action to a more leisurely pace, he looked around the room and gave the other people present a good chance to see his face. It was early in the afternoon and the scattering of other customers seemed too absorbed in their lunches to pay him any attention. He began to wonder if it would have been better to hide out in the city all day and visit the Blue Toad at night when it was likely to be much busier.

His deliberations were interrupted by the arrival of the waiter, who was wheeling a trolley upon which sat a small glass-sided aquarium. The tank was surrounded by a curious framework of glittering metal rods, forming a kind of cage, and in it – placidly scooting backwards and forwards in the water – was a pink crustacean about the size of Peace's little finger. He gazed at the tiny creature in bafflement for some time, then raised his eyes to the waiter, hoping to be enlightened.

'Your lobster, sir,' the waiter announced. 'Say when.' He pressed a switch which was connected to the cage by silvery wires and the entire assembly began to emit a faint humming sound.

'Hold on,' Peace said, pointing at the inhabitant of the tank. 'That thing's more like a shrimp. A baby shrimp, at that.'

'It's a baby Aspatrian lobster, sir.'

'But I want a grown-up one. A big one.'

The waiter smiled condescendingly. 'You can have it any size you want, sir – I'm growing it for you right now – but it's better not to let them get too old. It's a question of flavour.'

Peace watched in astonishment as the volume of space within the gleaming cage began to flicker in a disturbing way and the movements of the lobster in the tank abruptly speeded up. Suddenly he realized that the peripatetic shellfish was growing larger with every second. It was also becoming more complicated in shape, sprouting legs, pincers, feelers and eye-stalks in a profusion which would have shamed or terrified any Earth-type lobster.

'It's about two years old now, sir,' the waiter said helpfully. 'Some of our customers think that's when an Aspatrian lobster is at its peak, but others prefer them at three and even four years old. Just say when.'

'What's the . . .?' Peace swallowed noisily as he transferred his gaze to the cage surrounding the tank and saw that the gleaming rods of which it was built met at strange angles. They produced an odd wrenching sensation in his eyes when he tried to follow their geometries, almost as though they passed into another dimension. A bizarre idea was born in his numbed brain.

'That thing,' he said feebly. 'Is it a sort of time machine?'

'Of course, sir – all part of our gourmet service. Haven't you seen one before?'

'I don't think so,' Peace said. 'It was just that I noticed the way the rods meet at strange angles and create a wrenching sensation in my eyes when I . . .'

'I do beg your pardon,' the waiter said, looking concerned. He stepped back, studied the time machine with a critical eye, then grasped the framework in both hands and twisted it until it had assumed a conventional shape made up of square corners and rectangles. It continued humming away, quite unperturbed by the casual man-handling.

'The chef sat on it last week,' the waiter explained, 'and it hasn't been the same since.'

Peace wondered briefly if time machine technology was another significant area of his ignorance. 'I never expected to see a gadget like that.'

'Oh, this type – the single-acting introverter – is quite legal on Aspatria. Very useful for ageing whisky, but if you'll take my advice, sir, you won't let the lobster get any older.' The waiter switched off the time machine and, using a pair of tongs, hoisted the now enormous lobster up out of the tank. It eyed Peace malevolently, waving feelers and snapping its pincers.

'I'm not eating that thing,' Peace cried. 'It's a monster – take it away.'

'It will be killed, sir, and cooked to your . . .'

'I don't care! Take it away and bring me a steak.'

The waiter dropped the lobster back into the water and, mouthing silently as he did so, trundled the tank away in the direction of the kitchens. Peace made use of the extra time to study and be seen by the lunchtime customers and staff, but there were no visible flickers of recognition, no stirrings of his own memory, and he developed a gloomy certainty that he should have delayed his visit until the evening. The trouble was that, barring some kind of near-miracle, he would never be allowed inside the Blue Toad again.

When the steak came he ate it very slowly and, playing for time, became increasingly fastidious about every detail of the meal and the accompanying wines and liqueurs. The tactic had an unfortunate side effect in that, some-where around Peace's third demand for a different flavour of toothpick, the *maître de* correctly divined what was going on and stationed waiters at every doorway. To Peace's eyes these individuals seemed larger and more muscular than was strictly necessary for their calling. They gazed fixedly at him while the restaurant slowly emptied of cus-tomers, and inevitably there came the moment when he was alone with them in the large room. The floor waiter who had been serving him for the past two hours approached with an air of grim expectancy. He was carrying a tray of antique bakelite, in the centre of which was Peace's bill.

The waiter bowed stiffly. 'Will that be all, sir?'

'No.' Having given the only answer open to him, Peace tried to think of a suitable follow-up. 'No, that isn't all. Not by a long chalk. By no means is that all.'

The waiter raised his eyebrows. 'What does sir wish now?'

'Bring me . . .' Peace's brow prickled as he strove for inspiration. 'Bring me . . . the same again.'

'I regret that's impossible, sir.' The waiter placed the bill in front of Peace and folded his arms.

Peace turned the slip of paper over, saw that he had just spent the best part of a year's pay for a legionary, and experienced a chill sensation in his bowels. The feeling, while highly unpleasant, suggested a possible means of escape.

'Please,' he said, getting to his feet, 'direct me to the toilets.'

The waiter sighed loudly and indicated a panelled door at the opposite side of the room. Peace sauntered to it and, although he did not look back, received the impression that the covey of outsize waiters was closing in behind him. He went through the door, slamming it shut in his wake, and found himself in a small ante-room whose sole occupant was a dispenser robot which had about twelve gleaming arms, each one ending in a roll of toilet paper.

'I trust you have enjoyed an excellent meal, sir,' the robot said in an obsequious drone. 'My exhalation analysers tell me you dined on steak, and to complete your enjoyment I suggest a pliant but not unassertive paper such as our Superexec triple-ply pulped Lebanese cedar with the outer coating of . . .'

'Shove it,' Peace snarled, brushing aside the roll of pink tissue which zoomed towards him on the end of a telescopic arm. He opened another door and ran through into the toilets proper. There were cubicles on each side, and the opposite wall was spanned by a row of wash basins, above which was a single window. He started towards it eagerly, then saw that it was protected by massive bars which looked as though they had been designed to imprison angry gorillas.

Sensing that there was little time to spare, he dashed into the furthermost cubicle on the right hand side and locked the door. He removed his shoes and set them on the floor with their toes projecting a short distance under the door, and then – with an agility born of desperation – swarmed up the cubicle wall. He sprinted along the precarious stepping stones of the other partitions, not daring to think what would happen if he missed his footing, and dropped down into the cubicle nearest the toilet entrance. Its door was partly open and he crammed himself into the triangular hiding place behind it. A few seconds later multiple footfalls sounded outside, followed by an angry hammering on the cubicle door he had locked.

As soon as he judged that all his pursuers had passed him by, Peace darted out of cover and ran for freedom. There was an immediate outcry which had the effect of supercharging his muscles. He flitted past the dispenser robot, which was waving all its arms in a kind of mechanical palsy, burst out into the restaurant and headed for the exit. In the lobby he collided with the head waiter who, with a speed of reflex surprising in one of his age, grabbed a double handful of Peace's jacket.

'Got you!' he shouted triumphantly.

Peace kept on running, leaving the other man clutching a substantial area of blue paper suiting, and got safely into the street. The panorama of shuttling traffic and the footpaths crowded with shoppers was totally unfamiliar to him, but an instinct prompted him to turn left and he saw the entrance to an alley a short distance away. He reached it in several effortless bounds, almost as though propelled by his wayward Sevenleague boots, and glanced back.

'You won't get away with this,' the head waiter shouted from beneath the Blue Toad's entrance marquee. 'The police will get you. The Oscars will ...'

Snuffling with increased dread, Peace sprinted along the alley, turned several corners and saw a different street ahead. He slowed to a normal pace, stepped out into the late afternoon sunlight and did his best to mingle with the stream of passers-by – a difficult task in view of the fact that he had no shoes and a gaping hole in his jacket. It came to him that he needed to find a place where he could remain in concealment until darkness fell, and then take up a vantage point near the Blue Toad from which he could study the evening patrons. The best place for his purpose, he realized, would be a cinema, assuming that the ten monits still in his pocket would be enough to pay for an admission ticket.

The decision made, he walked cautiously southwards along the block, crossed to a lesser street on the opposite side and saw a cinema only about a hundred metres from the corner. Peace blinked several times, wondering how he had managed to find one so unerringly, and for the first time that day felt a glimmer of renewed hope. If he had known Touchdown City well in his previous life, it might be that exposure to the sight of his old haunts was beginning to rekindle his memory. Somewhat cheered by this notion, he approached the cinema and scanned its multifarious signs, looking for some indication of the admission charges. He quickly learned that it would cost him all of his ten monits to go inside, but other information presented on the placards seemed contradictory and confusing.

'GRAND FAMILY SHOW,' one sign read. 'THE VIOLENT VIR-
GINS – strictly for adults; with a fun-feast for the kiddies –
FLUFFO IN RAINBOW LAND.'

The building did not look big enough to contain two
separate auditoriums, and yet every sign plugged the same
message about a family entertainment which featured
both adult and juvenile films. Peace was frowning at the
bright lettering when he was approached by a blue-eyed
cherubic boy of about twelve. The boy was neatly dressed
in coppery shirt and hose, was shining with cleanliness
and radiated an impression of having been carefully
brought up in good surroundings. A paternalistic concern
about the child hanging around a dubious movie house
pushed Peace's own problems into the back of his mind.

'It will be dark soon,' he said, smiling. 'Why don't you
run home to mum and dad?'

'Why don't you,' the cherub replied, 'mind your own
bloody business?'

Peace's mouth fell open. 'Who taught you words like
that?'

'Who asked you to butt in?' The boy examined Peace
from head to foot, and his expression changed to one of
crafty appraisal. 'How'd you like to make fifty monits?'

'Don't be impertinent,' Peace said, affronted.

'It would buy you a pair of shoes – and all you have to
do is go into the show with me.'

'You're a nasty little whelp, and I wouldn't be . . .'
Peace's tongue went numb as he glanced further down the
street and saw a police car cruising slowly and watchfully
near the kerb. 'Let's go inside, sonny.' He walked into the
cinema foyer and jiggled nervously while he and the boy
bought tickets and were handed steribags containing what
looked like outsize sunglasses, a grey pair for him and a
yellow pair for the boy. The nose of the police car was
coming into sight as he pushed open the inner door,

anxious to reach the anonymous dimness beyond. Finding his way to a seat was easier than he had expected because the screen was so brilliantly lit that it cast a strong glow over the entire auditorium.

As he was walking down the central aisle Peace was puzzled to note that the too-bright screen displayed nothing but a meaningless confusion of images and that there was absolutely no sound track. Undeterred by what, to him, were serious flaws in the presentation, a hundred or more patrons were sitting in attitudes suggestive of rapt enjoyment. Peace began to get an inkling of what was happening when he realized that everybody, young or old, was wearing the same kind of peculiar sunglasses. Intrigued in spite of himself, he sat down beside his small companion and began to open the steribag given to him at the box office. The boy plucked it from his grasp and replaced it with the bag containing his yellow glasses.

'What's the idea?' Peace whispered.

'That's the deal.' The boy dropped a ten-monit bill into Peace's hand. 'I'll pay you ten an hour to a maximum of five hours.'

'But I don't . . .'

'Shut up and watch the pictures,' the boy said. He put on the grey glasses and settled back into his seat with a look of fierce concentration.

Peace stared at him resentfully for a second, then donned the yellow glasses. The screen instantly assumed a normal degree of brightness, showing a cartoon image of a fluffy kitten chasing a butterfly, and an appropriate soundtrack was fed into his ears via the side frames of the glasses. He watched the antics of the kitten for perhaps a minute, by which time intense boredom had set in, then he touched a miniature switch he had discovered on the bridge of the glasses. The cartoon film immediately changed with accompanying sound, to one in which an orange-coloured hound was unsuccessfully trying to scale a greased pole. Peace clicked the switch back and forth, and found that his choice was limited to the two equally depressing films he had already sampled. When he thought about it for a moment he realized that the lenses of his glasses were serving as stroboscopes, alternately becoming opaque and transparent at a frequency of perhaps a hundred cycles a second. Moving the switch altered the strobe timing, rephasing it and allowing the wearer to see a different film of the several which were being projected onto the screen at once.

He nodded in appreciation of the gadgetry involved – in an old-style cinema the audience was actually in darkness fifty per cent of the time, in between frames, and it was logical to use that time to project a different film. This explained the intense brightness of the screen when he had viewed it directly, without the filtering effect of the strobe glasses. Or did it? The screen had been *very* bright, with maybe four times the normal brilliance, and where were the violent virgins promised by the signs outside? At that moment cherub-face, seated beside Peace, gave a low moan of pleasure.

Peace regarded the boy suspiciously, then snatched the grey glasses away from him and crammed them on to his own nose. He was assailed by an orgiastic panorama of heaving flesh, plus sound effects which made it clear that if any of the participants really were virgins their departure from that blessed state was imminent. A feeling of warmth spread over Peace's face.

The boy tugged at his arm. 'Give me back my glasses.'

'I will not.' Peace took the glasses off and folded them up.

'But I paid you for them.'

'I don't care,' Peace said firmly. 'There ought to be a law against showing that sort of thing to minors.'

'There is, poop-head. Why do you think I'm paying you? Come on – hand them over.'

'Nothing doing.' Peace offered the boy the yellow glasses. 'You'll have better fun watching Fluffo.'

'Balls to Fluffo,' the boy retorted. 'Look, mister, hand over the glasses or I'll make trouble for you.'

Peace sneered at him. 'After what I've been through, you think you can make trouble for me!'

'*Leave me alone,*' the boy screamed. 'Stop touching me! Go away!'

'Just a minute,' Peace said, alarmed, 'perhaps we can ...'

'No, I don't want to look in your grown-up glasses – they show awful things happening. Please don't make me look.' The boy's voice grew even louder, convincingly hysterical. 'I just want to see Brown Houn' and Fluffo. Take your hand away! What are you doing to me?'

'If you don't keep quiet,' Peace whispered, brandishing his fist. 'I'm going to smash your evil little face.'

'Is that a fact?' a gruff voice said close behind him. Powerful hands lifted Peace right out of his seat and suddenly he was being propelled up the aisle with his arms twisted behind his back. Women in the end seats he passed hissed abuse at him and made painfully accurate swings with their handbags. Peace tried to break free, but his captor was too strong for him and seemed to have had training in physical combat. He opened the heavy swing doors by the simple expedient of bouncing Peace against them, and then both men were out in the foyer. A managerial-looking woman with silver-blue hair and a pince-nez came out of a side office, drawn by the sounds of commotion.

'Got one, Miz Harley,' Peace's captor announced. 'Child molester. Caught him in the act. Now can I have a bonus?'

Peace wagged his head earnestly. 'This is ridiculous. I never touched the boy. I was only ...'

'Shut up, you.' The big man shook Peace reprovingly,

giving him a mild case of whiplash. 'I saw him, Miz Harley. Caught him in the act. About my bonus, Miz Harley, do you think...?'

'Perhaps we ought to hear what the gentleman has to say about it,' Miz Harley said in reasonable tones which were music to Peace's ears. She came nearer, adjusting her pince-nez. Her eyes focused on Peace's face and the colour abruptly fled from her cheeks.

'It's *you*,' she said in a scandalized voice, taking a step backwards. 'Up to your old tricks! Is no child safe from you?'

'What is this?' Peace protested, too shocked to feel any satisfaction at apparently having found a link with his past. 'I wouldn't dream of...'

Miz Harley pointed an accusing finger into his face. 'You've tried to disguise yourself! The beard makes you look different, but not different enough. You've been here before, interfering with children. You're a *monster*!'

Not again, Peace thought, as the familiar words echoed in his mind. He put on what he hoped was a smile, and said, 'Look, can't we talk this over quietly in your office?'

Miz Harley shook her head. 'It's people like you who give simultaneous cinemas a bad name.' She transferred her gaze to the big man behind Peace. 'Blow your whistle, Simpkins.'

A large hand carrying a subetheric whistle appeared at the edge of Peace's field of view, and a moment later there came a piercing warble which he sensed to be loaded with all kinds of ultrasonic frequencies. People on their way into the cinema paused to whisper to each other and to examine Peace with obvious distaste. His shoulders drooped as he realized that his spell of freedom was drawing to a close. The police were on their way, and in a matter of minutes he would be handed back to the Legion, having learned no more about himself than that, apparently, he had a history of molesting children. Perhaps he was a monster, after all – in which case he deserved everything that was coming to him.

'There are quite a few Oscars in town today,' Miz Harley said comfortably. 'I'll bet they get here first.'

'Hope they do – the police is too soft.' Peace's captor gave him another shake. 'We should've thrown all these Earthie Blue-asses off the planet altogether in '83. I blame the Government, of course. What was the point in us beating the tripes out of them in the war, and then letting them walk all over the place terrifying innocent kiddies?'

'Innocent kiddy!' Peace was stung to protest, although the mention of Oscars had chilled his blood. 'That little swine was ... Wait a minute! *We* won the war in '83.'

'Oh, yeah?' The big man gave a rumbling laugh. 'It looks that way, doesn't it? You don't see our boys going about with no shoes. You don't see our boys going around dressed in trampy fourth-rate gear.' Warming to his subject, he transferred his hold to the shoulders of Peace's jacket. 'Look at this stuff, Miz Harley. Why, it's no better than ... *paper*!'

The break in the big man's rhetoric was occasioned by the fact that Peace, on the instant of feeling the restraints transferred from his person to his clothing, had begun to run for the cinema exit. There was a loud ripping sound and his jacket, already seriously weakened by the day's escapades, disintegrated entirely. Clad in only a half-sleeved shirt and lightweight hose, he darted out into the street and, with a curious feeling that all this had happened to him before, turned left and ran like a gazelle, scarcely feeling the ground beneath his feet. He made ready to fend off busy-bodies who might try to interfere with his escape, but his progress along the narrow thoroughfare was strangely unimpeded. The late afternoon shoppers, who would normally have been intrigued by the sight of a partially clad man fleeing through the city had drawn close to the walls and were staring at something further along the street in the direction in which Peace was running. He narrowed his eyes against the low-slanting rays of the sun, and promptly skidded to a standstill, his mouth contorted by shock.

Coming towards him, the light glinting on the enormous bronze muscles of their shoulders, were two Oscars.

Peace had no recollection of having seen similar beings in the past, but neither had he any difficulty in matching them to Dinkle's description. The hairless domes of their heads and overall metallic sheen of their nude bodies were unmistakable, as were the massive torsos which tapered down to lean hips and powerful thighs. They paused in their effortless loping run, appeared to confer for a second or two, and then – as if they truly were telepathic and could see into Peace's soul – ran towards him, glaring with terrible ruby eyes.

'Oh, God,' Peace quavered. He remained transfixed with terror for what seemed an eternity before leaping sideways into an alley which emerged between two stores. The adrenalin-boosted fleetness he had shown earlier was as nothing compared to the superhuman speed he now developed within a few windmilling strides. Aware that he had to be breaking the galactic sprint records, Peace risked a backwards glance and saw that the long stretch of alley was still deserted. He was beginning to feel a glow of self-congratulation when the wall just behind him burst asunder in a shower of bricks and the two Oscars, who had cheated by taking a diagonal shortcut through the building, appeared at his heels.

Peace emitted a falsetto scream and went into a kind of athletic overdrive which took him beyond the reach of grasping metallic fingers. He caromed around a corner and saw, a short distance ahead of him, an oddly familiar doorway above which was a faded sign reading: ACME RAINCOAT CO. He flew to it, burst open the door and ran up a dark flight of stairs. He paused on a shabby landing and saw before him yet another door which was labelled in barely decipherable letters, 'Female Toilets – Acme Employees Only'.

I refuse to hide in any more lavatories, he thought, but at that instant the outer door to the building crashed open with a splintering sound and the two bronze figures came pounding up the stairs, their eyes glowing redly in the dimness.

Peace shouldered his way into the toilets, and realized at once that he was trapped. The tiny room in which he found himself was filthy and disused, obviously a century old or more, and had no other exits. Its sole illumination came from a cobwebbed skylight which, even had he been able to reach it, was too small to clamber through. He turned, clutching at a last straw, to bolt the door – but discovered he was too late.

The Oscars were already standing in the doorway, stooping to peer at him below the lintel.

Peace backed away from them, dumbly shaking his head. His heels encountered a projection on the floor and he sat down with bone-jarring force on the ancient toilet seat.

A curious humming noise filled the room and – before Peace's petrified, disbelieving eyes – the menacing figures of the Oscars became transparent and faded into thin air.

chapter seven

Peace ogled the empty doorway for several pounding seconds, wondering what had happened to the bronze giants. It seemed impossible for such massive figures to become insubstantial and then vanish entirely, but there was no denying the evidence of his own eyes. Or was there?

As the shock of his strange reprieve began to wear off, Peace's awareness of his surroundings grew more acute and he realized that peculiar things were happening all around him in the little room. The walls and ceiling were beginning to look cleaner and fresher, cracks were disappearing from the plaster, and the paintwork – contrary to the natural order of things – was renewing itself, and even changing colour.

There was a pervasive energetic humming noise and the light from the overhead window was flickering in a disturbing way. Peace gnawed his lower lip as he tried to connect the last two effects with something in his previous experience. A picture of a baby Aspatrian lobster scooting around in a tank sprang into his mind, and he gave a moan of dismay as a full understanding of his predicament swiftly followed.

The two Oscars had not faded into nothingness. They had remained solid, securely anchored in the year 2386, while he – Warren Peace – had faded out of *their* sight.

He was adrift in a runaway time machine!

'This can't happen to me,' Peace said aloud, obstinately shaking his head, but his brain was dredging up other pertinent memories. The waiter in the Blue Toad had described his portable time machine as a single-acting introverter, which implied the existence of other types, among which might be a double-acting extroverter – whatever that was. If an introverter altered the rate of time within its framework and left the outside world unaffected, an extroverter might – Peace struggled with unfamiliar concepts – maintain a normal time flow internally and cause the external universe to age or grow younger. The phrase 'double-acting' suggested that an operator had the choice of going backwards or forwards in time, but Peace was not operating the machine he had blundered into. He had no idea of where its controls were, nor of the temporal direction in which he was travelling, nor why anybody should have been crazy enough to secrete a time machine in a raincoat factory toilet in the first place.

Impelled by a needling sense of urgency, Peace jumped to his feet, and in that instant the humming noise ceased and the light in the room steadied to a normal glow from above. He turned and looked thoughtfully at the rickety toilet seat, then dismissed the notion that it might contain a pressure switch which activated the time machine when anybody sat down. His world had gone haywire recently, but there had to be a limit somewhere. Anxious to get out of the device's sphere of influence, he strode out on to the landing and looked around. The building was quiet, but it now had a lived-in atmosphere which, together with the improved conditions of its fabric, suggested to Peace that he had journeyed into the past. The question was – how far?

Bemused and still trembling from his exertions, he opened a door to his left, listened to make sure there were no sounds of occupancy, and went into a large room which seemed to be equipped for some kind of scientific research. Peace, who had half-expected to see rows of sewing machines, paid little attention to the scattering of instrument cabinets, cables and electrical chassis. He went to a business calendar on a wall nearby, looked at it and felt a sudden weakness in his knees. The date it quoted was 2292, which – if he accepted the figure – meant he had gone back 94 years into history.

Peace placed a hand on his brow and tried to make a new assessment of his situation. How was he going to regain knowledge of his past when that past was now in the future? What chance had he of, say, ever being reunited with his father and mother when they had yet to be born?

He glanced around wildly and spotted a newspaper lying on a work-bench. It was covered with fragments of what appeared to be a pork pie, which he shook off on to the floor. The date at the top was: 3 June 2292 – confirming the information he had gleaned from the calendar. He was gazing at the numerals in utter despondency when he heard the door to the laboratory being thrown open.

'Put your hands in the air,' a man's voice told him. 'And don't try anything funny because I've got a gun pointing straight at your fourth vertebra vertebra.'

Peace raised his hands resignedly. 'Look, I'm not a thief.'

'I'll be the judge of that,' the man said. 'It seems to me you're acting like a thief thief.'

'Stealing a lousy newspaper!' Peace cried, irritated by the fresh injustice that fate was heaping on him, and by his unseen captor's nervous tendency to repeat the last words of sentences. 'Big deal!'

'I might have jotted down some valuable formulae on that paper paper.'

'Had you?'

'No, but you weren't to know that. Turn around and let me see your face.'

Peace gave a loud sigh and turned round. The small, rotund, red-and-ginger man who was covering him with a pistol gave a visible start of surprise.

'It's you you,' he whispered.

'Of course.' Peace was no less surprised, but he retained enough presence of mind to seize the initiative. 'Who am I?'

'Don't you know?' the little man said, seizing the initiative back again.

'Of course I do – I just wanted to see if you knew.'

'How would I know? I've never seen you before in my life.'

'But when you saw my face just now you said, "It's you."'

'I didn't.'

'Well, actually you said, "It's you you."'

'Mock another person's afflictions, would you?' A look of contempt appeared on the little man's florid countenance. 'I thought that sort of callousness died out in the nineteenth century.'

'I'm not mocking,' Peace said impatiently. 'I'm just telling you what happened happened.'

'At it again, are you?' The little man brandished the pistol under Peace's nose. 'I'm not afraid to use this, you know know. Who are you, anyway?'

'You should know if you've met me before.'

'I've never met you – you just look a bit like somebody I once knew. Now, what's your name?'

'Warren Peace.'

'That doesn't sound like a real name to me,' the little man yelped angrily, growing even redder. 'I'm warning you – cut out the funny stuff.'

'It's my name – at least, I think it is.' Peace tried to keep a tremor of self-pity out of his voice. 'You see, I've lost my memory.'

'A likely story!'

'It's true.'

'More likely you're a spy, trying to steal my ideas. You know who I am, don't you? Professor Armand Legge, the inventor.'

'How can I know who you are if I don't even know who I am?' Peace said with some asperity. 'I tell you, I've no memory of my past life.'

Legge stared at him for a moment, and gradually the look of hostility on his face was replaced by one of intemperate delight. 'I know what to do,' he said, beaming. 'Why didn't I think of it before! I'll put you into my truth machine. This is an ideal chance to try it out.'

'Truth machine? Try it out?' Peace stared back at Legge with a slow-dawning fear that he had strayed into the clutches of a mad scientist. Legge looked like a jovial monk, with his tomato cheeks and fringe of saffron hair, but appearances could be deceptive, and for all Peace knew his captor was a maniacal experimenter who took out people's brains and popped them into jars of formaldehyde as casually as a farmer's wife pickling onions. His curious speech defect, which made him sound like a robot whose voice mechanism was slipping a cog, could very well be an indication that he was totally inhuman.

'You can't put me into any machine,' Peace answered firmly. 'There's a law against that sort of thing.'

'But who's going to find out?'

'The Oscars will . . .' Peace lapsed into silence, realizing the futility of threatening Legge with the attentions of creatures who would not come into existence for almost a century.

'Don't worry – it will be quite painless. Just take off your clothes and sit down over there.' Legge used his revolver to point into a corner of the room at a machine which Peace had not previously noticed, but which bore a disquieting resemblance to an electric chair.

Prodded by the gun muzzle, he stripped off the remnants of his clothes, sat down on the wooden seat and allowed his forearms and ankles to be encircled by heavy straps. Legge then produced a chromium helmet which was connected by wires to a small console, and placed it on Peace's head. Whistling cheerfully, he opened a drawer in a work-bench and took out a lacy pink brassiere, the left-hand cup of which had been filled with miniature electronic components. He fastened the brassiere around Peace's chest and spent some time carefully positioning the equipment it contained. Peace's apprehension increased as Legge set up around the chair a portable framework to which were attached six small gas cylinders whose nozzles were pointed straight at him, and which could be operated by a single lever.

'Let me go,' Peace pleaded, abandoning his pride. 'I'll never trouble you again if you let me go.'

'My dear boy, this is no trouble. In fact, I'm quite enjoying myself.'

'I'm not,' Peace said.

'Hardly the point, is it? Anybody who sneaks into a research laboratory deserves all that's coming to him.'

'But I thought this was a raincoat factory. It says so outside.'

'Everybody knows I bought this place when Acme folded up a couple of years ago, so I'm not much impressed by that excuse.' A fanatical gleam had appeared in Legge's eyes as he made some final adjustments to his equipment. 'Enough of this shilly-shallying! It's time to prove that the Legge truth machine is another invention worthy to take its place alongside the Legge mem . . .' The little man broke off and clapped a hand over his mouth as though he had almost committed a serious indiscretion.

'What were you going to say?' Peace said, his interest aroused.

'Nothing. Nothing at all all.' Legge hurriedly threw some switches on his console and gripped the lever which controlled the six gas cylinders. 'Ten, nine, eight, seven, six . . .'

'What are you going to do to me?' Peace said nervously.

'The first step is to override your psychogalvanic reflexes,' Legge replied. 'Five, four, three, two, one one.' He pulled the lever down hard and there was a loud hissing noise as the cylinders discharged their contents in Peace's direction.

'Not the gas! I can't stand gas!' Peace struggled with his bonds as clouds of grey vapour enveloped him, then he paused, incredulously sniffing the powerful aroma of cheap scent. 'Hey, this smells like Rambling Rose Country Fresh Deodorant.'

'That's what it is,' Legge said. 'I'm sorry about the smell – but there was a special offer on the stuff at the supermarket round the corner. Treble stamps, too.'

'But . . .' Peace gave a shaky laugh. 'Why a deodorant?'

'That part's incidental – I'm only interested in the antiperspirant effect.'

'I don't get you.'

'To override your psychogalvanic reflexes, dummy. You know the principal of the conventional lie detector, don't you? It works because when the subject tells a lie he experiences an emotional stress which makes him sweat – thereby increasing the electrical conductivity of his skin. The same stress speeds up his heart and changes his brain rhythms. A polygraph is able to detect all those things and indicate when the subject is lying, but that's only one half of the job. I mean, detecting a lie isn't as good as being told the truth, is it?'

'I'm not sure,' Peace said.

'Of course it isn't! So what I've done is to put the lie detector system into reverse. Right now it's impossible for you to sweat, because your pores are full of antiperspirant; your heart can't speed up because there's a super-pacemaker strapped over it; and that helmet you're wearing is forcing all the EEG patterns of your brain to remain normal.

'So, when I ask you a question, you – denied all the ancient psychological accompaniments to a lie – will only be able to respond with the truth. Ingenious and subtle, isn't it?'

Peace was unimpressed. 'What happens if I refuse to say anything at all?'

Legge picked up his gun. 'In that case – I shoot you.'

'That's *very* ingenious and subtle,' Peace said drily. 'I hope you realize this is a complete waste of time – I've no reason to hide the truth.'

'Don't lie to me.'

'How can I when I'm in your truth machine?'

'I forgot forgot.' Legge looked flustered at being caught out. 'You think you're pretty smart, don't you, Norman?'

'No, I don't think I'm . . .' Peace gave the other man a penetrating stare. 'Why did you call me Norman?'

'Um . . . I thought you said your name was Norman.'

'I'm supposed to be a complete stranger to you. You're supposed to believe I'm a thief or a spy – and yet you want to be on first name terms with me. That doesn't make much sense, Professor. Come on – admit you've met me before. Admit you know who I am. Admit that you . . .' Peace stopped himself in full spate, partly because he had leaned forward, determined to achieve a logical victory, and a jet of deodorant had gone straight up his nose, causing him to sneeze and somewhat diminishing the effect of his oratory; partly because he had just remembered he was now in an era in which, strictly speaking, he had not even been born. It was difficult to see how Legge could have known him previously, and yet . . .

'What's the matter, egghead?' Legge jibed. 'Tripped over your own terminology, have you you?'

'Why did you call me egghead?' Peace said, still tantalized by the faint hope that he might be close to the solution of all his problems. It occurred to him that he should aim to get free and, assuming the contraption worked, strap the professor into his own truth machine. He decided, as a matter of policy, to start ingratiating himself with his captor.

'I don't like eggheads,' Legge went on. 'Just because somebody goes on to university for a few years and picks up a few degrees he thinks he knows more than a plain man who left school when he was fifteen.'

'Ridiculous notion,' Peace said.

'Let me tell you, I'm as good a scientist and inventor as anybody. You know, it wasn't a high IQ and fancy education that made Einstein a great scientist. It was his simple and childlike approach to problems – and my approach is probably even simpler and more childlike than his was.'

'I've no doubt it is.'

'Thank you.' Legge looked mollified, then the stern expression returned to his face as he remembered the serious nature of the business in hand. 'On with the interrogation – what's all this about you having lost your memory?'

'It's true, Professor. I don't know who I am. As far as I'm concerned, life began about a month ago.'

'Mmmmph.' Legge glanced at his console and nodded. 'I thought that sort of thing only happened in movies. Any idea what made you lose your memory?'

'Yes. I joined the Space Legion to forget something, and they wiped out my whole past life.'

'The Legion!' Legge became animated. 'I see! I see! They've only been doing engram erasure for a year or so. Probably bungled your case.'

Peace shook his head. 'I joined in 2386 – and by that time they'd had nearly a century of experience with the equipment.'

'But that's . . . um . . . ninety-four years in the future!' Legge cast an inadvertent glance towards the landing where the toilet was situated. 'Did you . . .?'

'Yes. I was being chased, and I ran into this building –

I don't know why – and hid in the toilet. Next thing I knew I was here in 2292, and you were pointing a gun at me.'

'It has happened again,' Legge said in a doleful voice. 'Old Smirkoff has a lot to answer for.'

Peace frowned his puzzlement. 'Who's Smirkoff?'

'Dimitri Smirkoff – the meanest man on Aspatria.' Legge began switching off his machine, apparently satisfied with Peace's credentials. 'He built an illegal time machine and hid it in the toilet. The cage is concealed in the walls walls.'

Peace's bafflement increased. 'But why would anybody do a nutty thing like that?'

'Smirkoff owned the raincoat factory, you see. It churned him up that he had to pay the girls for the time they spent in the toilet, so one Christmas when he had the place to himself he came in here with a time machine kit, built it round the toilet and replastered the walls so nobody would notice. I'm told he even tried to cut the girls' production bonus to pay for the redecorating. Talk about *mean*!'

'But what was the idea?'

'Well, the machine was an extroverter – the sort that only Government agencies are allowed to operate. Smirkoff's idea was to set it up so that no matter how long anybody spent in the toilet – reading, smoking, talking – when they came out only one second of external time would have elapsed elapsed.'

'Good grief!' Peace was astounded by the misguided ingenuity. 'Still . . . it must have improved his output figures.'

'That's where you're wrong, my friend. The moron – not having any scientific understanding – set the machine up all wrong. It became unstable, erratic, and girls started disappearing. The place got the reputation of being haunted, nobody would work here any more, and Smirkoff went out of business. That's how I was able to buy the building for my research work.'

'Can't you deactivate the machine? Turn it off?'

'Are you kidding?' Legge began unfastening the straps around Peace's ankles. 'To get at the master control I'd have to go inside, and there's no way I'm going to risk being a castaway in another century. I'm not mad, you know know.'

'Shouldn't you at least nail the door shut?'

'That wouldn't prevent people materializing in there from another time and maybe starving to death.' Legge's rubicund features wrinkled in distaste. 'How'd you like to work beside a closet full of dead bodies?'

'Not much,' Peace admitted, looking all around him with growing interest now that the immediate threat to his well-being had receded. The laboratory, although badly disorganized, contained a great deal of expensive equipment, and it occurred to him that any inventor or private researcher who could afford to buy an entire factory building for his work had to be a very successful man. It was difficult to reconcile that conclusion with the general demeanour of Legge himself, who seemed as mad as a hatter, but perhaps the man could be crazy and brilliant at the same time. Peace flexed his fingers gratefully and stood up as the straps fell away from his forearms.

'This is quite a place,' he said. 'What sort of work do you do?'

Legge stepped back from the chair and picked up his gun. 'Do you think I'd be mad enough to tell you?'

'But I thought we'd established that I'm not a spy.'

'Is that any reason for me to tell you the things a spy would want to find out?'

'I guess not.' Not wanting the little man to become any more nervous and twitchy while he had a gun in his hand,

Peace decided to steer the conversation on to neutral ground. He unfastened the pink brassiere from around his chest, held it up and whistled in mock admiration.

'With a bit more work,' he said, 'you'll be able to get the whole machine into this thing.'

'You filthy over-sexed swine!' Legge cried, his face changing from red to a dangerous puce. 'How dare you insult my daughter!'

'Professor, I didn't know . . .'

'Disgusting, that's what it is.' Legge waved the gun, its muzzle tracing a circle of menace. 'I've done my utmost to shield my little baby, my pretty little child, my sweet innocent little . . .'

'She can't be all that little,' Peace said reasonably, trying to take the emotional heat out of the situation. 'I mean . . .'

'My God, is there no end to your lasciviousness and lechery? Even with a gun pointing at you, all you can think about is the size of . . .' Legge stopped in mid-sentence and a new light of determination appeared in his eyes as he steadied his aim with the pistol. 'I've had all I can stand of you. This is where we say goodbye goodbye.'

Peace cowered back from him. 'You can't shoot an unarmed man.'

'Don't you believe it.' An ominous coldness had appeared in Legge's voice. 'Come on – start walking.'

'Where to?'

'Back into the time machine, of course. My daughter will never be safe while you're around.'

'You can't put me back into that thing. You can't be that inhuman.'

'Start walking walking.'

Peace glanced around in desperation. 'At least let me put my clothes on.'

'Do you think I'm a fool?' Legge said. 'The old "Do you mind if I have a cigarette?" ploy won't work with me –

I've been to the movies too many times, junior. You press a button on your cigarette case and it squirts tear gas into my eyes. It's a cunning trick, but it isn't going to work this time, because I'm too smart for you you.'

'I don't want a cigarette,' Peace replied. 'I just want to put my clothes on.'

'And squirt tear gas at me from a shirt button? Get moving!'

Peace started walking towards the door, with Legge behind him. On reaching the workbench near the door, he tried to salvage something of his dignity by picking up the newspaper he had previously examined, shaking the last crumbs of pork pie from it, and wrapping it around his middle. He allowed himself to be shepherded along the landing, but paused at the toilet door, his dread of the unknown overcoming his concern about what Legge might do to him if he refused to go inside.

'Listen,' he said, turning to face the little man, 'we're quite a distance above the ground on this floor – and I think you should give some thought to what will happen if I go back to a time before this building was constructed.'

'All right, I'll give it some thought.' Legge mused for a moment, and a smile appeared on his face. 'I like it! I like it!'

'You're willing to see me fall to my death?'

'Unfortunately I'll be denied that spectacle. In any case, the time machine is probably going through a phase of damping oscillations – they're inclined to do that, you know. You'll probably come out in the future near the time you went in.'

'You're just guessing,' Peace accused. 'Anyway, I've got a feeling you wouldn't have the nerve to pull that trigger, so . . .'

'So?'

'So I refuse to go into the time machine.'

Legge shrugged. 'It's your funeral.' He cocked the pistol, giving a very good impression of a man who was preparing to commit murder. Peace, beginning to suspect that he had made a very serious misjudgement, took an involuntary step backwards. There was a nerve-racking pause, at the end of which the gun muzzle began to waver uncertainly. Peace exhaled quietly with relief.

At that instant footsteps sounded close by on the stairs leading to the upper floor, and a large, pink female version of Professor Legge came into view, bristling with hair curlers and billowing with quilted nylon.

'Oh, Daddy,' she said in an incongruous baritone, 'you've taken my best bra again for your silly old . . .' She stopped speaking as she espied Peace, a look of incredulous joy spreading over her features, and she lumbered towards him with arms thrown wide. 'Norman, you've come back to me!'

Peace's reaction was completely instinctive.

He leapt backwards into the toilet, lost his footing and sat down hard on the decrepit wooden seat. There was a loud humming noise, the light began to flicker, and the bulbous figures of Professor Legge and his daughter faded from view in the doorway. Peace gave a moan of apprehension as he realized that – clad in only a newspaper – he was once again voyaging through time.

chapter eight

Under Peace's fascinated scrutiny the walls of the little room began to exhibit colour changes.

One of his major worries was removed when he saw that the general condition of his surroundings was deteriorating. This meant he was travelling into the future and that the building was not going to leave him in mid-air by snapping out of existence. He relaxed for a moment, glad of the breathing space in which to sort out his jumbled thoughts, then came the realization that all buildings are eventually torn down. If he went too far into the future he could either be dashed to the ground or, worse still, find his body bisected by one of the walls of a replacement building.

Alarmed and aggrieved by the way in which life had been reduced to a succession of leaps from frying pans into fires, Peace hurriedly got to his feet, and at once the aural and visual effects of time travel ceased. The glow from the dusty skylight held steady once more, and to Peace's eyes the room looked exactly as it had done when he first saw it. He glanced towards the door, half expecting to see two dreadful bronze-gold giants glaring at him with ruby eyes, but the landing outside was deserted. The stillness would have been tomb-like but for the faint murmur of city traffic outside.

Holding his improvised kilt in place around his loins, he advanced cautiously on to the landing. A thick layer of dust lay over everything, and it gave Peace a crawling sensation on the nape of his neck when he realized that Legge and his daughter, alive only one subjective minute ago, had probably seen out their allotted spans and now were resident in grave or funeral urn. He turned left, opened a door and went into the large room he had known as Legge's laboratory. Some of the workbenches were still in place, but the jumble of equipment – with the exception of some small items and wiring – had long since been removed. Gazing around the time-ravaged walls, Peace tried to assimilate the items of half-knowledge he had gained.

Professor Legge's daughter had recognized him, and she too had addressed him as Norman. Did this mean that his name really was Norman? Or was it an alias he had used in a previous trip into that era? What reason could he have had for doing that? If Professor Legge had known him, why had he tried to disguise the fact? Come to think of it, how could he be sure he was not actually a citizen of the late twenty-third century who had somehow been displaced into the late twenty-fourth century? Had he been running from the law in the twenty-third century, too, and been forced to flee into the future? What crime had he committed? Was he – unbearable thought – really a confirmed molester of small children, as the cinema manageress had stated?

The practical side of Peace's nature suddenly made him aware that he was wasting his time in futile speculation, and that his primary requirements were clothing, money and an accurate fix on his position in time. He opened several closet doors and was scarcely able to believe his luck when he found, hanging on a rusted nail, a once-white coat of the type favoured by laboratory workers. It was much too short, but a full search of the room's storage spaces yielded no further treasures. He moved upstairs and while touring the empty living rooms discovered a pair of fluffy bedroom slippers which, judging by their size, could once have belonged to Legge's daughter. They were on the verge of disintegrating with extreme age, but fitted him quite well and gave his feet some measure of protection. The complete ensemble was, Peace felt, somewhat lacking in elegance, but it was possible that if the building had not acquired the reputation of being haunted the local urchins would have stripped it bare, and he would have been left in a similar condition.

Reminded of the method by which small boys traditionally supplemented their incomes, Peace thought of the miscellaneous scraps of hardware languishing in the dust of the laboratory. One of the items had been a bunsen burner which, for all he knew, might have acquired the status of a semi-antique since it was last in use. He rushed back to the big laboratory, spread out his newspaper and collected on it a heap of copper coils and small pieces of electronic junk. The bunsen burner had a solid, well-crafted feel to it and, although it was not in the same class as a nineteenth-century brass microscope, Peace could imagine a trendy collector getting quite excited over it.

He wrapped his plunder up in a bundle and went out of the laboratory and down the stairs to street level. After a brief struggle with a rusty shootbolt, he opened the door and stepped out into a cool purple twilight. The alley was deserted, but the sound of traffic told him the business life of the city was still in full spate, which meant the season was either spring or autumn, and that the time was late in the afternoon. He turned to the right, away from the street where he had seen the Oscars, and headed for the opposite side of the block.

On reaching the corner he peered out cautiously and was relieved to note that the passing vehicles looked very much as he remembered them – an indication that he had not jumped to a distant era of the future. The lighted store windows looked reassuringly normal, as did the pedestrians who hurried by Peace without sparing him a glance. Emboldened, he joined the flow of people and began searching for a likely antique shop. His progress was impeded by the shuffling gait he had to adopt to make the fluffy mules stay on his feet, and to his horror a playful breeze kept lifting the hem of his lightweight coat, forcing him to stop every now and again to tuck the garment between his legs. Doubled over, clutching his parcel, unable to raise his feet or separate his knees, Peace was uncomfortably aware that he looked like a skulking transvestite Quasimodo – a sight which, even among the most blasé city-dwellers, was bound to excite comment.

As he had feared, men and women began to stop to watch him pass by. He tried grinning at them to create the impression he was a harmless idiot, but within a short time he was being followed by a knot of interested spectators. The nightmarish feeling intensified as he realized the police were bound to become involved sooner or later. He was preparing to stand up straight and make a run for it, regardless of the amount of exposure involved, when he noticed a sign a few doors further along which said: *R. J. PENNYCOOK – Antique Dealer*. Filled with relief, he scuttled towards the discreet-looking establishment, darted inside and slammed the door behind him. He leaned against it, breathing heavily, feeling like a fox which had just been delivered from a pack of hounds.

'If you don't get out of here immediately,' said a cold-eyed young man, from behind a glass counter, 'I'll send for the police.'

'You can't do that to me,' Peace gasped, shaking his head.

'I'd like to know why not.' The young man picked up a subetheric whistle and raised it to his lips.

Peace glanced around him and his heart sank as he saw he had taken refuge in a shop which catered for the extreme top end of the market, the sort of place where Ming vases are thrown in free with the really expensive purchases. Suddenly his corroded bunsen burner seemed to have lost its cachet, but he could think of no other course than to brazen the matter out and play for time.

'For the simple reason, Mr Pennycook,' he said impressively, advancing to the counter, 'that I've got something to sell, something whose value you may not appreciate at first glance, but the like of which may come your way only once in a lifetime.' He set his parcel on the counter and spread it open, revealing what – even to his eyes – looked like a shovelful of scrap metal. Even the bunsen burner, pride of the collection, had separated into its constituent parts.

Pennycook looked down at the miscellany. The faint trace of colour that had been in his cheeks promptly disappeared, and within the space of a second his expression changed from one of disdain – through incredulity, joy and greed – to a look of respectful wariness. 'Is this yours to sell?'

'Of course.'

'Where did you get it?'

'Just picked it up.' Peace, who had been watching the play of emotion on the dealer's face, began to wonder if he had stumbled on to a craze for old bunsen burners which would guarantee him enough money for a second-hand suit. 'There could be more where that came from,' he added encouragingly, tapping the side of his nose.

'I'll give you a thousand for it,' Pennycook said briskly. 'No questions asked.'

'A thousand!' Peace began scanning the small mound of salvage, trying to see each grubby piece with the sort of unbiased eye which could identify hidden riches.

'All right, two thousand – but that's my top offer. Is it a deal?'

Peace swallowed with some difficulty. 'It's a deal.'

The young man took two large and colourful banknotes from a drawer and handed them to Peace. He then carefully gathered up the bunsen burner and other items and dropped them into a waste disposer. There was a flash of greenish atomic fire as the objects ceased to exist.

'What are you doing?' Peace said, shocked at the casual destruction of what he had begun to see as an art treasure.

'We don't need them any more,' Pennycook said. 'It was a good idea to wrap the paper round some old junk – the old stealing of wheelbarrows trick, the old purloined letter ploy – but you could have got it dirty.' He smoothed the newspaper out with reverent hands, examined it closely and looked up at Peace with a shocked expression. 'If I didn't know better, I'd almost think somebody had been eating a pork pie off this.'

'Never!' Peace said numbly.

'I suppose you're right. Nobody in his right mind would desecrate a mint, laser-imprimed, Waldo-folded 2292 newspaper.' Pennycook gave Peace a conspiratorial glance. 'It's a long time since I've seen a specimen as good as this – it's almost as if you'd got hold of an extroverter and gone back for it.'

'But that sort of thing is illegal,' Peace said, winking in an effort to pass himself off as a useful source of contraband. The mentality of the dedicated collector was foreign to him, but – now that he finally understood the situation – he was determined to take every advantage it offered. 'Listen, Mr Pennycook, do you . . .'

'Call me Reggie, please.'

'Okay, Reggie – I'm Warren – do you think we could go into your office and talk? I feel a bit awkward standing around with practically no clothes on.' Acutely conscious of the thinness of his legs, Peace endured a head-to-foot perusal of his body.

'I've been meaning to ask you about that – I have to be very discreet, you know,' Pennycook said. 'How did you lose your clothes?'

'Well . . .' Peace was stumped for a suitable reply. 'You know how it is.'

Pennycook's brow cleared. 'I get it! Say no more, Warren.'

'I won't,' Peace assured him.

'Her husband came home unexpectedly and you had to run for it, you randy old jack-rabbit.' Pennycook gave Peace an amiable punch on the shoulder. 'I don't mind telling you, Warren, when you came in here dressed like that, and reeking of that awful rose perfume, I thought you were . . .'

'How dare you!'

'It's all right – now that I know you better I can tell you're a bit of a stud.'

Peace was nodding his agreement when a disturbing new thought crossed his mind. He could divine within himself no interest whatsoever in the opposite sex, which seemed curious in the case of a healthy young man who had had no physical gratification in over a month. *I've been too tired,* he decided, pushing aside memories of how all his comrades in the Legion – despite exhaustion and malnutrition – had spent their scant leisure planning the orgies of the next leave period. Frowning, and more than a little subdued, he followed Pennycook into an office at the rear of the premises.

'Have you any idea how I could get some clothes?' he said. 'I don't mind what it costs.'

Pennycook nodded. 'The Ten Monit Tailors is a few doors along the block. I could ask somebody to bring you a suit and some other things.'

'Ten monits! That's not bad.'

'It'll be more like a hundred – inflation, you know.' Pennycook turned away with a humorous glance at Peace's bare legs. 'You really are a randy old jack-rabbit, Warren.'

'Don't keep saying that,' Peace replied irritably, not wishing to be reminded of the vast new areas of unspeakable sin which might lie in his past. He glanced around the office and his attention was caught by an electronic calendar which announced the date as 6 September 2386. The red-glowing figures blurred in his vision and came back into sharp focus as he suddenly grasped their significance. If the calendar was accurate, it meant that the time machine – in one of the damping oscillations about which Professor Legge had spoken – had dropped him off at a point *two months before he had joined the Space Legion*.

A weakness developed in Peace's knees as, with a thrill of almost superstitious awe, he realized that his mysterious former self was alive in some other part of the galaxy at that very moment, no doubt busily adding to the mountain of guilt which would eventually drive him to the Legion's recruiting office and the memory eraser. The concept, inured to shock though he was, threw Peace into a mental spin.

'I'll call the tailors now,' Pennycook said, sitting down at his telephone. 'Fix you up in no time.'

'Thanks,' Peace said abstractedly. 'By the way, is your calendar right?'

'Why? Don't you know what day it is?'

'It's not that.' Peace strove to orient himself in the present. 'I've been travelling a lot and I'm losing track of the time zones.'

'We use a compatible local calendar to match the Aspatrian seasons,' Pennycook said. 'If you want the date on Earth it's . . . let me see . . . the eighth of November.'

Peace sat down abruptly, his legs giving way altogether as it came to him that – simply by lying in wait outside the Legion recruiting station in Porterburg, Earth, in two days' time – he would be able to meet the one person in the universe who could answer all his questions.

chapter nine

A night's sleep in a comfortable hotel bed, the feeling of being clean and well fed, the knowledge that he was properly dressed and had money in his pocket – all these should have improved Peace's frame of mind as he set out to walk to the spaceport in Touchdown City.

Instead, his brain used its renewed energies to dredge up further hints at his abnormality. Not only did it appear that he had an unsavoury reputation as far as small boys were concerned, but there was the curious business of Professor Legge's daughter and the time machine. He, Warren Peace, had defied death at gunpoint rather than step into the machine – and yet he had willingly *thrown* himself into it to escape the embrace of a woman. The only crumb of comfort he could derive from his memory of the incident was that the female concerned had resembled a two-metres-tall amorous blancmange. Perhaps, Peace speculated, he would have reacted differently had she been young, slim and pretty.

As he walked through the crisp brightness of the autumn morning, Peace put himself to the test by staring long and hard at every attractive girl he saw among the city crowds. He derived a certain aesthetic pleasure from their appearance, but to his disappointment felt none of the stirrings he believed appropriate to a recent member of the brutal and licentious soldiery.

The experiment came to an abrupt end when, in his anxiety for results, he failed to observe that one subject was accompanied by a bull-necked heavyweight of jealous disposition who spun on his heel and made a grab for Peace's collar. The agility Peace had developed in a dozen battle zones got him out of what could have been a nasty situation, but he decided not to risk drawing any further attention to himself.

He was not scheduled to join the Legion until the following day, which meant he was not now being hunted as a deserter – nor had he yet done any of the other things which were to get him into trouble – so it seemed advisable to keep his nose clean until he got safely to Earth. The civil spaceport was further away than the hotel clerk had given him to believe, and Peace began to regret his decision to walk. On impulse he hailed a passing taxi. The yellow car pulled to a halt at the kerb beside him and its window slid down to reveal the lugubrious countenance of Trev, the driver who was destined to have the same window beat in on top of him by Peace a month later.

Peace instinctively covered his own face with his hands and hissed, 'Go away! Why don't you leave me alone?'

Trev's face twitched with indignation and he accelerated off along the street, mouthing silently.

Unnerved by the brief encounter, Peace made himself as inconspicuous as possible during the remainder of the walk. Ten minutes later he reached the spaceport and was surprised to find it was only about the size of a large sports stadium, and had a similar kind of architecture. So many spaceships were continuously arriving and departing that the air above the field was darkened by a huge spout-shaped cloud of blurred dumb-bells. Peace was shocked by the magnitude of the traffic control problems involved, until he noticed that the ships' trajectories criss-crossed through each other at will, and it dawned on him that the peculiar form of locomotion the vessels employed, in which they were neither in one place nor another at any given instant, meant it was impossible for them to collide.

He nodded his approval, conceding that – ugly though the cubist spaceships were compared to his visualized gleaming spires – they were an excellent mode of transport. He went into a ticket office, paid four hundred monits for a one-way trip to Earth, and emerged into a lounge which provided a panoramic view of the myriad ships actually landing and taking off. Craning his neck to take in more of the scene, he shouldered his way towards the low barrier at which the customs scanners were positioned, and had almost reached it when he became aware of bronze-gold reflections hovering at the edge of his field of vision. He turned and found himself looking at two Oscars who were calmly strolling among the knots of passengers and sightseers.

Peace's instinctive reaction was to flee – his feet were making preliminary movements of their own accord – but his intellect dictated otherwise. Running would be the surest way of drawing attention to himself, and there was the overriding consideration that he was not guilty of any offence. There was no way of telling if these Oscars were the same pair who had chased him in his subjective yesterday – their smoothly cast features were almost identical – but the point was that this was the ninth of November, and therefore his desertion from the Legion, his abscondence from the Blue Toad, and the embarrassing episode at the movie house all lay a month in the future. Even if the Oscars could read minds, as some people had said, they could not persecute them for crimes they had yet to commit. He took a pack of self-igniting cigarettes from his pocket, sucked one into life and tried to appear relaxed and unconcerned.

The Oscars continued on their course through the departure lounge, the morning light glinting on tapering muscular bodies, their ruby-eyed faces impassive. People moved respectfully out of their way, but otherwise hardly seemed to notice the presence of the statuesque beings. Wishing that he could be similarly unconcerned, Peace tried to blank out all memory of his misdeeds and discovered that resolving not to think of any particular subject produces an effect opposite to the one intended.

He pursed his lips and began to whistle tunelessly, a trick he felt would make him the image of bored innocence, but had forgotten his lungs were full of cigarette smoke. He emitted a single, hacking cough, loud as the bark of a walrus, which caused some bystanders to start violently and drew glances of sympathy from others.

The Oscars turned their heads towards him, and both came to a halt.

Peace, trying to stare down the inhuman gazes, puffed faster at his cigarette. *I'm not guilty*, his mind chanted in panic. *I haven't done all those awful things.*

The Oscars' heads rotated slowly until they were looking into each other's eyes. Their silent communion lasted for several seconds, then both nodded and came striding towards Peace. So determined was he to prove he had nothing to fear that he waited until they were almost upon him before his nerve broke. Ducking to avoid outstretched brazen arms, he bolted for the only open ground available, which happened to be the landing field itself. He reached the customs barrier and, his muscles again supercharged by fear, sprang cleanly over it and headed out into the haphazard alleys formed by the parked spaceships. A clangor of falling metal behind him announced that, characteristically, the Oscars had chosen to run straight through the barrier. Their footsteps drummed loudly in his wake, growing closer with every microsecond.

Peace cast around wildly for an escape route and saw a dark rectangle which was an open door at one end of a spaceship. He dashed into it, slammed the heavy steel door into place; to his relief, it locked automatically. Grateful for the fortress-like protection of the ship's armoured shell, he staggered across what appeared to be a control room and dropped into its single cushioned seat. Breathing noisily, struggling to repress the trembling of his limbs, he surveyed his new environment and tried to plan his next move. The attempt at cerebration ended, stillborn, as one of the loudest sounds he had ever heard reverberated through the square room and, in the same instant, a bulge the size of a dinner plate appeared on the door he had just closed.

Peace's face contorted with shock as he deduced that one of the Oscars had punched the steel slab with his fist – *and had almost succeeded in holing it*. With fingers crammed into his mouth, he stared in horror at the distorted metal and realized that had the Oscar thought of striking near the lock the door would almost certainly have burst open.

Perhaps, he thought, avidly clutching a thread of hope, *they aren't very intelligent. Perhaps that's their one weak point, their Achilles' heel. If so, how can I turn this fact to my advantage? How can I . . .?*

Again his powers of thought were swamped by a cataclysmic sound, a second bulge appeared on the door, and it was borne home to Peace that the Oscars simply had no need for brain power. They were invincible as they were. Driven almost beyond reason, he swung round to the sloping control console at which he was seated. A curious ripple passed over his vision, accompanied by a pins-and-needles sensation within his head, and for a fleeting moment he saw the array of instruments and controls through the eyes of another person. He stroked his hand down two rows of toggle switches, hit a large red button, and pulled upwards on the central control stick.

The blank wall in front of him became transparent. There was a glimpse of the spaceport buildings falling away below, a flash of blue sky turning to black – and then he was gazing, transfixed, at the hard, hostile brilliance of the stars.

*

The speed of the ship was so great that Peace could see a flowing change of parallax in the nearer stars. Entranced by the spectacle, he watched the bright specks swimming by; then it occurred to him that in order to produce such an effect the ship had to be going like a bat out of hell – and he had no idea of where it was headed. He should have been overjoyed at once more being delivered from the hands of the Oscars, who seemed to bear him a grudge, but now there was a new danger of his being lost for ever in the deeps of space. It was beginning to seem that there was no end to the unpleasant surprises fate had in store for him, that no matter how many catastrophes he avoided there would always be more lying in wait . . .

'That's it,' Peace said in an aggrieved voice. 'What's the point of struggling? I'm just going to sit here and accept my destiny – and what a strange and lonely destiny it's going to be!

'On and on I'll go,' he intoned, warming to the subject, 'far beyond the meagre confines of this galaxy and all the galaxies about it. Outstripping the speed of laggard light, on laughter-gilded wings, I'll suffer a C-change. And what marvellous sights I'll see before death finally closes my eyes – nebulae writhing in the exquisite torment of crea-tion, the cosmic beacons of supernovae, universes like fireflies tangled in a silver braid . . .'

Pleased with his newfound fatalism, Peace crossed his arms, sat back in the deep chair and made ready for etern-ity. He remained at one with the cosmos for perhaps ten seconds, and then boredom set in. It was quickly followed by panic.

'Bugger the fireflies and silver braid,' he cried, leaping from the chair. 'I want to go home.'

He ran to the transparent front wall and hunted all over it, as though having moved two paces closer could help him identify the pinpoint of light which would be

Sol. Even in his distraught condition he realized almost at once that the quest was hopeless – there were millions of suns, scattered ahead of the ship in such profusion that it was impossible to impose any kind of order on them. Nothing short of a powerful computer would be able to cope with the astrogation problems involved, he decided, and caught his breath as the pins-and-needles he had experienced earlier returned in force, causing a strange *easing* sensation within his head. It was rather as if a tourniquet had been relaxed, except that the renewed flux was far less tangible than blood, consisting as it did of an ethereal slurry of associations, ideas and concepts.

Am I getting my memory back? he wondered, returning to the spaceship control console. *Have I ever flown a ship like this?*

He sat down and examined the various panels more carefully, this time beginning to appreciate that there were a number of logical groupings. The rows of switches he had thrown in his first flash of perception had labels which identified them with transceiver warm-up and manual take-off, but there was a separate module, resembling a typewriter keyboard, at the top of which was a plate engraved with the letters A.D.S. Reasoning, prayerfully, that they stood for Automatic Destination Selector, he tapped out E-A-R-T-H and was rewarded by an immediate rotation of the star fields ahead, evidence that the ship was changing course. A red circle began to blink in the middle of the transparent wall. It was enclosing one of the few tiny areas of absolute blackness visible to him, and he realized he was so far from Earth that the light from its parent sun had been unable to make the journey. But even as he watched, a mote of light appeared at the centre of the circle and began to grow brighter.

Satisfied that things had begun to go better for him, he studied the other modules and found one labelled Autoland – which disposed of his worries about setting the ship down safely. Emboldened by his success and growing sense of familiarity with the controls, he switched on some music. The first minitape he tried yielded an orchestral recording of a piece by Sibelius, the ponderous cadences of which might have been designed as mood music for stargazers.

He sighed approvingly and relaxed into the deep cushions, determined to make the most of a calm interlude. Now that he was assured of the partnership being purely temporary, he again permitted his soul to unite with the cosmos, and – to add a visual garnish to his meditations – flicked toggle switches which caused the remaining walls of the control room to become transparent. As is often the case with artistic final flourishes, the move proved to be a serious mistake as far as his peace of mind was concerned.

Only a few paces away to his left, the upper surfaces of their bodies reflecting red and green pulses from the ship's marker lights, the two Oscars clung to the outside of the hull.

I've killed them, Peace thought, terrified. *I've dragged them into interstellar space and killed them!*

His fear abated, only to return tenfold, as he saw that – incredibly – the enigmatic beings were still moving.

Showing no signs of discomfort in the airless void, they were holding on to the ship with casual one-handed grips while pointing out celestial landmarks to each other, like tourists on a pleasure trip. Peace stared at them, petrified. Every now and then one of the Oscars would turn slitted ruby eyes in his direction – apparently without seeing him. He guessed the transparency of the hull was a one-way effect.

Peace's brow furrowed as he got a new inkling of the forces arrayed against him. Life had been difficult enough before the Oscars had come on the scene to hound him through time and space – now he learned they were indestructible, apparently capable of surviving anywhere under any conditions. The impossibility of visualizing what he had done to deserve such relentless pursuit added to Peace's misery. He lowered his face into his hands and thought seriously about ending the persecution by driving the ship into a sun. It would be a quick, clean solution to all his problems, but – a single crystal of resentment formed and began to grow in the cauldron of his mental turmoil – was he prepared to accept it at this eleventh hour? After all he had endured in the past month, was he going to allow two metallized morons to prevent him learning the truth about himself?

He raised his head, sat up straight and began to analyse his new predicament. The Oscars had obviously been within the field generated by the transceiver towers at each end of the ship, which was why they had been carried into space with it. Ryan had taught him that the vessel could be regarded as being at rest, in spite of possessing an effective velocity, which meant there was no inertia and made it easy for outside passengers to remain in place. He was positive, however, that the fierce accelerations of 'normal' space flight would quickly dislodge any unwanted joyriders.

The ship's target sun, Sol, was already growing brilliant in the forward screen as he turned his attention back to the control console. He found a panel labelled AUX. NUC. PROP. MODE, and with growing assurance identified it as a set of controls for flying the ship on nuclear propulsion when the main system was inoperative. His fingers positioned themselves naturally on the altitude selectors and the miniature joystick, and he knew in the instant that he had flown spaceships at some time in his previous life, and that he could make the one he was in perform any manoeuvre he wished.

Snorting with triumph, he shut down the transceiver drive and the ship – which had been travelling at millions of kilometres a second – immediately came to a halt. It did so without a tremor or jolt, the fact that it had no inertia making the abrupt change of condition unnoticeable.

A glance to his left confirmed that the two Oscars, quite unawares, were nonchalantly holding themselves in place by their fingertips. A look of gleeful malice spread over his face as he made ready to blast the ship forward under full normal acceleration. He touched the firing button – and his expression changed to one of dismay as he found himself unable to depress the concave disk. No matter how many commands he gave his finger it refused to move.

'This is crazy,' he said aloud, staring accusingly at the dissident digit, trying to reason with it. 'Those things out there aren't even human. I mean, they're *monsters*.'

Lots of people say you're a monster, he could imagine the finger replying, *but you didn't like the idea of being marooned in space, did you?*

'Listen to me, knucklehead,' Peace argued, 'those characters get their kicks by feeding helpless men to their pet throwrugs.'

You've only got Dinkle's word for that – and, anyway, since when did two wrongs make a right? You can't do it, Warren. You can't inflict that fate on anybody or anything.

'All right, all *right*!' Peace glowered helplessly at his finger for a moment, then revenged himself on it by poking it into his nose.

With his left hand he activated the transceiver drive and in less than a second the ship was again travelling Earthwards at a speed of several hundred light years an hour. The Oscars continued to float beside the hull in weightless relaxation, red and green highlights flowing like oil on their massive torsos.

Peace transferred his attention to the forward screen and noted that the point of searing brilliance which was Sol had grown into a disk. It began to drift to one side of the winking red circle – an indication that the ship was now homing in on Earth – and he knew he was running out of time in which to solve the problem posed by the Oscars. Unless he did something quickly he was going to find them hammering the spaceship's door to pieces as soon as he touched down.

As if to illustrate the urgency of his plight, a blue-white orb appeared in the target circle and ballooned outwards until it was recognizably the planet Earth with the escorting Moon peeping over its shoulder. On the control console a sign lit up advising Peace to feed details of his chosen landing point or go over to manual control. He stared in perplexity at the broad blue curvatures of the mother world for several seconds before deriving inspiration from its predominant colour.

Taking control of the ship, he steered a course down through the atmosphere, pleased by the absence of re-entry effects, and slanted towards the middle of the Pacific Ocean. The descent was comparatively leisurely, giving him plenty of time to look for a suitable dumping ground. He found a group of small atolls, brought the ship to a halt in the air about a hundred metres above a lagoon, and – after taking a deep breath to steady his nerves – switched off the transceiver drive.

The ship fell like a lead weight.

Peace counted two seconds and fired the nuclear drive, with dramatic effect. As the thrusters came into play, the plummeting ship clanged as if it had struck an invisible barrier, and Peace – who had been perched on the edge of his seat – was forcibly driven down on to his knees, catching his chin on the edge of the console. Nursing his jaw, which felt as though it had been unhinged, he looked to

137

the left and in spite of his pain was overjoyed to see that the Oscars had disappeared.

The ship's structure was creaking and protesting as the thunderous nuclear jets bore it aloft again. Peace put the metal giant out of its misery by making a rapid switch back to the transceiver mode, and swung into a curve for a slow pass close to the atoll. Ripples were still spreading across its central lagoon, but he could see down into the clear water without difficulty. The Oscars were standing on the floor of the lagoon, unperturbed at being under several fathoms of water. Their faces tilted upwards as they watched the spaceship cruise by overhead, and it seemed to Peace that they were shaking their fists at him.

'Same to you, fellers,' he called. 'Watch out for rust.'

Chuckling with satisfaction, he boosted the ship high into the afternoon sky and set a course for Porterburg, the city he presumed to be his home. In an older type of craft the navigational problems would have been considerable, but Peace simply flew in a sharp climb until he had reached orbital height – a manoeuvre which took only ten seconds – and could see the entire western seaboard of the North American continent laid out beneath him. From there it was easy to pick out the estuary of the Columbia River, in the middle latitudes of the long narrow Republic of Califanada which stretched from Mexico to Alaska. He could also see the planetary terminator sweeping in from the east, and knew the short winter's day was drawing to a close in Porterburg and Fort Eccles.

Cool intangible fingers stroked his spine as he realized that his previous self was down there at that moment, preparing to carry his burden of remorse for one more night before making the fateful visit to the Legion's recruiting station. It briefly occurred to Peace that *he* had no intention of joining the Legion and therefore no longer required a lever to get him out of a service contract. The wisest thing might be to steal away quietly and allow his past, with all its guilt, to remain a mystery. He flirted with the notion for a moment, then shook his head and put the ship into a steep descent. Unhampered by inertial and aerodynamic effects, the vessel reached the vicinity of Porterburg in some twenty seconds.

As the city appeared on the forward screen, an accretion of silvery cubes on a broad bend of the Columbia, he remembered he was now guilty of stealing a spaceship and was likely to be arrested if he put down at any civil or military landing field. Making a snap decision, he overflew Porterburg by about forty kilometres and selected a snow-covered pasture which was reasonably close to a small community, but screened from it by low hills. The ship settled with a jolt and the control room door slid aside to admit a gust of chill November air.

Peace stepped out into the silent twilight and took his bearings. Bordering the field was a second-class roadway which looked as though it ran straight to the community he had noticed from the air. There was nobody in the area who could have seen his arrival, and within a matter of minutes darkness would cloak both the spaceship and Peace's subsequent movements. A comforting sense of being in command of the situation burgeoned within him as he realized that all he had to do was play it cool until the morning, avoid attracting any attention, and – above all – control his tendency to become involved in silly accidents. Turning up his collar, he squared his shoulders and set off walking towards the road.

'Just a moment, young man,' a woman's voice called imperiously. 'Where do you think you're going?'

Peace froze in his tracks, his eyes wide with disbelief, and turned around.

The door in the ship's central passenger section had sprung open and, almost filling it, was a stout, middle-aged woman wearing a straw sun bonnet and a flowered dress. Other portly and middle-aged ladies, similarly attired, milled about behind her in the lighted interior, emitting bleats of consternation. Peace staggered like a man who had been sandbagged as he realized he had stolen a ship which was full of Aspatrian passengers.

'See that?' another woman said, joining the first in the doorway. 'He's drunk! I *told* you the pilot was drunk. Coffee all over me I've got, and it's all his fault.'

'Where are we anyway?' a third chimed in. 'This doesn't look like the Sunnyside Weight-free Pleasure Asteroid to me.'

'I'm sorry, I'm sorry,' Peace mumbled, backing away. Gradually gaining speed until he had reached the safe maximum for that form of perambulation, he turned and ran as fast as he could. The party of stout ladies watched until he had faded out of sight in the gathering dusk before turning to each other with looks of indignation. Silence reigned for several seconds, and then – by mutual consent – they produced subetheric whistles from their purses and blew a long and concerted blast of pure outrage.

Five thousand kilometres away to the south-east, where the afternoon sun was still shining on a Pacific atoll, two gold-gleaming supermen – who had been staring irresolutely at the sand – suddenly raised their heads. They remained in a listening posture for a time, red fire pulsing in their eyes, the hairless domes of their skulls reflecting the sun's brilliance.

At last the giants turned to each other, nodded, and ran down a sloping shelf of coral into the sea. Too heavy and compacted for swimming, they continued to run along the ocean floor after the water had closed over their heads, and sea creatures prudently darted out of the way as the invaders of their domain struck a course for Califanada.

*

Panting loudly with exhaustion, Peace leaped over a boundary ditch and reached the verge of the deserted highway. Snow which had been cleared from the road itself formed a low moraine on each side. Slithering over this last barrier with some difficulty, Peace brushed snow and ice droplets from his clothing, shoved his hands in his pockets and began walking in the direction of the nearby settlement.

Everything is still all right, he assured himself. *Those old trouts on the ship are bound to be a bit upset, but they don't know how lucky they are I changed my mind about going far beyond the meagre confines of this galaxy and all the galaxies about it, and the suffering a C-change bit. That would have really given them something to complain about! Anyway, it will be hours before they can contact the police, and in the meantime I've got plenty of money for transport, I'm correctly and inconspicuously dressed, I'm close to Porterburg, and I'm fit and healthy – except for a suspected fracture of the lower mandible, and perhaps some frostbite.*

All I have to do now, he impressed on himself, building up his confidence, *is stop being so damned accident prone. Play it cool! Blend into the background! Even I can stay out of trouble till the morning.*

The concentrated dose of positive thinking had an immediate effect on Peace's spirits. A certain amount of spring returned to his stride and a few minutes later – as though honouring the promise of divine assistance for those who help themselves – the lights of a bus appeared in the distance. As the vehicle drew closer Peace saw that its destination was Porterburg, and he breathed a sigh of gratitude. He signalled the driver to stop and, avoiding any possibility of having his toes flattened by a wheel on the narrow road, mounted the glassy bank of snow and waited until the bus had drawn up in front of him. Its doors opened with a pneumatic gasp. Peace edged forward, his feet shot out from under him, the icy surface hit the back of his head and, with no perceptible lapse of time, he found himself lying, hands still in pockets, in pitch darkness under the bus. Metal components churned dangerously near the tip of his nose as he struggled to get his hands free of the pockets, which had suddenly developed a vice-like grip on his wrists.

'Where did that joker go?' The bus driver's voice could scarcely be heard above the noise of machinery, but it had a distinct note of impatience.

'I'm down here,' Peace croaked. 'Help me, somebody!'

'People flag you down, and then it turns out they don't want a ride after all,' the driver grumbled. 'I don't know – it must be a new craze.'

There came the sound of doors closing, the bus rolled forward and its nearside wheel brushed the hair on top of Peace's head. He was congratulating himself on, at least, having escaped a gory death when a projection near the vehicle's rear end struck him in the ribs and trundled him along the ground for a short distance before releasing him in an untidy heap in the centre of the road.

Peace struggled to his feet, clutching his side, and swore at the departing bus. When its lights had finally vanished into the night, he looked down at himself and was aghast to see that his jacket and hose, immaculate only a short time earlier, were oil-stained and torn. He giggled hysterically for a moment, then clapped a hand over his mouth.

'I'm not going to let this thing throw me,' he announced to the lonely expanse of moonlit snow all round. 'I am the master of my own destiny.'

Taking stock of his physical condition, he found he could still walk although, in addition to a contused jaw, he now sported a throbbing lump on the back of his head and at every breath was experiencing a sharp pain which suggested one or more broken ribs. Travelling by public transport no longer seemed a good idea, in view of his appearance, but he had enough money to go by taxi to Porterburg and find a discreet hotel. After a shower and a night's recuperation, he told himself, he would be almost as good as new. The first essential was to find a telephone, and from there on everything would be straightforward. Drawing the tatters of his jacket closer around himself, Peace once again set out for the nearby community, which – in spite of its geographical proximity – was beginning to seem as distant and unattainable as Shangri La.

Twenty minutes later he passed a sign which read, 'HARTLEYVILLE – Pop. 347', and limped down the single main street in search of a telephone kiosk.

Although it was early in the evening the street seemed deserted, and consequently he felt a pang of irritation on reaching a phone box to find that not only was it in use, but that there was another prospective caller waiting to get in. Reminding himself of the need to be philosophical in the face of such minor annoyances, Peace took his place in line and hoped his condition would not attract any comment. He need not have worried on that score, because the red-haired man in front – hardly sparing him a glance – was devoting all his attention to hammering on the door with his fist and shouting abuse at the man inside. It appeared he had been kept waiting for some time and, lacking Peace's hard-won stoicism, was nearing a state of apoplexy. He kept darting from one window to another, making gestures of frustration and rage, but the dimly-seen caller within foiled him each time by turning away, as users of call boxes have done since time immemorial.

Peace watched the little drama with Olympian amusement, pondering on the pettiness of the troubles which some mortals allowed to disrupt their serenity. He was beginning to wish he could drop a hint about what real misfortune was like when the red-haired man uttered a climactic burst of obscenities, scurried across the street and disappeared between two buildings. Less than a minute later the man in the box finished his call, came out, nodded to Peace and faded away into the night, leaving him free to make use of the telephone.

Patience does it every time, Peace thought smugly, stepping into the box. He had just begun to conjure up information about taxi services on the illuminated directory display when the door was yanked open behind him. A rough hand dragged him out into the open and he found himself gazing up into the flinty countenance of a very large and cold-eyed policeman. The red-haired man had returned to the scene with the policeman and was hopping up and down in the background.

'That's him!' he said vindictively. 'Twenty minutes he kept me waiting out here in the cold. Run him in, Cyril, run him in!'

'Do me a favour, Reuben,' the cop replied. 'Don't try to teach me the job, huh?'

'But *twenty minutes*, Cyril! Everybody knows you're only allowed three minutes in a public call box.'

'Pardon me, officer, but this is all a mistake,' Peace said, his heart sinking. 'I've only been here a minute and . . .'

'*Liar!*' Reuben screamed. 'He's trying to con you, Cyril. He thinks you're a dumb hick cop.'

'Is that a fact?' The policeman gave Peace a stare in which the hostility was augmented by dawning suspicion. 'How did you get all messed up like that? What's your name, mister, and where are you from?'

'Me?' Peace spoke with the calmness of desperation. 'I'm from nowhere.'

Summoning reserves of strength whose existence he had not suspected, he gave the policeman a violent shove in the chest. The big man, taken unawares, lost his footing on the packed snow and fell on his back with an appalling crash of harness and equipment. Peace leapt over him and fled into one of the alleys which had begun to feature so prominently in his affairs, running so swiftly that he felt at one with the night wind, scarcely aware of his feet touching the frozen ground.

A stabbing pain in the side of his chest brought him to a standstill in a very short time, the effortless dream-flight at an end. He looked all around in the darkness. He could see nothing but moon-silvered trees and flat snowscape beyond, and there were no sounds of pursuit. Sitting down on a convenient tree stump, he waited for his mind to catch up with his body. Though it appeared he was safe for the minute, he found it chastening to reflect that within half an hour of setting foot on Earth he had contrived to injure himself, ruin his new clothes, and get into fresh trouble with the law.

There's no doubt about it, he thought, adding to his little store of self-knowledge. *I'm quite definitely accident prone.*

The revelation prompted him to make a tough reappraisal of his plans. As his breathing gradually returned to normal there came the conviction that his only hope of keeping the morning appointment lay in getting to Porterburg alone and unaided – which meant he would have to walk all night. The prospect was a daunting one, especially as the air was growing noticeably colder by the minute, but all other options had retreated or vanished.

Aching from head to toe, already beginning to shiver, Peace lurched to his feet and began the dismal forty-kilometre trek he hoped would end at the crossroads of the past, present and future. His bout of philosophizing while waiting for the telephone already seemed pathetic, but he made a last effort to locate at least one positive aspect of the situation, to find a nugget of hope which would sustain him through the night. At first the task seemed quite impossible – then his thoughts focused on the single, glittering achievement of the day.

'Thank God,' he said fervently, hobbling through the snow, 'I managed to shake off those damned Oscars.'

chapter ten

His month in the Space Legion had familiarized Peace with hardship and discomfort, but in retrospect – by the time he reached Porterburg – it seemed a halcyon period of comradeship, laughter and warmth.

He inched through the city in the steely light of dawn, trying not to draw attention to himself, but at intervals was overtaken by trembling fits so violent that his torn clothing flapped audibly, giving him something of the demeanour of a drug-crazed Haitian dancer. Most of the early morning pedestrians hurried by with averted eyes, but a few were stung to compassion and approached him with offers of money or help. Where possible he quickly sent them on their way with hoarse assurances of his well-being, but two persistent cases had to be frightened off by deliberately going into the voodoo routine with extra conviction. This was strangely easy to do, and before long he was forced to accept the idea that he could be suffering from pneumonia.

Death itself had begun to seem quite an attractive prospect, but the idea of it occurring before he had completed his mission filled him with alarm. Coaxing his limbs to make greater efforts, he speeded up his progress and eventually reached the quarter of the city wherein lay the headquarters of the Space Legion's 203 Regiment. He turned into a mean and rather narrow street and saw before him a large redbrick building, reminiscent of a brewery, which bore a sign proclaiming it to be Fort Eccles. The structure in no way resembled Peace's conception of a Legion establishment, but he had passed the stage of caring about such anomalies. He went along the side of the building, inspecting various doors until he reached one which had a plaque identifying it as the entrance to the recruiting office.

In spite of his chronic debility, Peace's heart quickened as he realized that this was the exact location of his second birth a few crowded weeks earlier, and that the solution to the great mystery of his life was almost within reach.

A notice on the door yielded the information that the office would be open for business at 8.30 a.m. Peace no longer had a watch, but had passed a number of clocks in the district. He knew he was approximately an hour too early, and that waiting that length of time in the intense cold could easily be the last nail in his coffin. He glanced about him and almost sobbed with gratification as he espied an orange-lit bar directly across the street. Its steamy windows promised heat and sustenance, and furthermore would provide a vantage point from which he could monitor all arrivals at the recruiting office. Bitter experience had taught Peace that it was always when his fortunes appeared to be taking a turn for the better that disaster struck him yet another blow, but he was unable to repress a glow of simple pleasure at the prospect of a comfortable seat, heated air and pots of strong, scalding coffee. Clamping his arm against his damaged ribs, he shuffled across the street and went into the bar, which was almost empty at that hour of the day.

The bartender eyed him speculatively, but immediately became affable when he set a fifty monit note on the counter. A couple of minutes later, armed with a beaker of coffee stiffly laced with Bourbon, Peace made his way to the front of the narrow room and dropped into a chair at the window. He sipped his drink eagerly, holding the container in both hands, absorbing every calorie. So intent was he on the life-giving brew that half of it was gone before his eyes could focus on anything further away than the beaker's rim. He found himself staring at another early-morning customer – a clean-shaven young man with a doll-pink face, wide mouth, blue eyes, and blond hair which was fashionably thinned above the forehead. The young man, slumped in his seat, was the personification of hangdog misery – exactly as Peace had last seen him, projected as an image on the wall of Captain Widget's office.

A tidal wave of hot coffee washed around Peace's nostrils as he realized he was looking at himself.

Not daring to think about the complexities which lay ahead, he got to his feet and limped to the other table. 'Mind if I sit here, Norman?'

'I don't mind.' His other self continued to stare into an empty glass.

Peace sat down. 'Don't you want to know how I know your name?'

'Couldn't care less.' The young man raised his head and regarded Peace with mournful eyes which betrayed not the slightest trace of recognition. His gaze shifted to Peace's grubby hands and disreputable clothing, and he took a crumpled ten-monit note from the pocket of his brown houndstooth jacket. 'You should buy food with that – not booze.'

'I don't want a handout.' Peace pushed the bill away, and decided to try shock tactics. 'Norman, what would you say if I told you that you and I are the same person?'

'I'd say you ought to lay off the vanilla extract for a while.'

The leaden indifference in his other self's voice shocked Peace, but he pressed on. 'It's true, Norman – just look at me.'

Norman gave him a cursory glance. 'You don't even look like me.'

Peace opened his mouth to argue, and at the same instant caught a glimpse of himself in a wall mirror. He appeared ten years older than Norman, was much thinner, bearded, ragged, filthy, and had a swollen jaw which substantially altered the shape of his face. He also had a black eye, which he had not known about until that moment, and the harsh night of exposure had imparted to the rest of his skin the sort of blue-red hue normally acquired through a strict diet of cheap wine. Peace gulped and had to admit that Norman was right – they looked like two different people.

'All right,' he said, pouring sincerity into his voice. 'I've been through a lot lately, but I tell you it's true – you and I are the same person.'

A hint of amusement appeared briefly on Norman's doom-laden countenance. 'This is the weirdest come-on I've ever heard, and it's being wasted – I've already given you the money.' He pushed the note back across the table.

'I don't want your money,' Peace said impatiently, wondering how he could ever have been so obtuse. 'Are you going to listen to me, Norman?'

Norman sighed and glanced at his watch. 'I suppose it will help to pass the last hour – conundrums instead of cognac. Why not? Let me see now, this must be like that old one about proving to somebody he isn't here, except that I've to guess how you and I can be the same person. How about . . .?'

'You don't have to guess anything – I'm going to *tell* you.' Peace sipped some coffee to hide his exasperation. 'Supposing I tell you I've been in a time machine, and that . . .' He broke off as he saw that the fresher version of himself was dogmatically shaking his head.

'I wouldn't believe you. Double-acting extroverters are illegal – especially here on Earth where there's so much more history to be interfered with. Government detector vans go around all the time and root them out as soon as they're switched on. I've heard they can even tell what year you're tuned in to.'

'That's the whole point,' Peace said triumphantly. He was on the verge of explaining that he was talking about an event which had occurred on Aspatria when a mind-quaking new thought stilled his voice. He had been so busy trying to bring this meeting about that there had been no time to plan what he was going to say, or in which to think about the possible consequences. Norman had been to Aspatria already, that much he knew, and if he now named the planet in evidence, convinced Norman he was speaking the truth, and went on to catalogue all the horrors and miseries of the last month – Norman could very well decide not to join the Legion.

And he, Warren Peace, was the individual who had come into existence as a direct result of Norman signing on for his thirty, forty or fifty years !

Peace hurriedly swallowed some more coffee as he tried to sort out the paradoxes involved. If Norman changed his mind about entering the Legion, would Warren Peace cease to exist? Somehow the notion of being erased by a shift in probabilities was more terrible to Peace than that of facing a straightforward, old-fashioned death. A man who was dying normally had the consolation of knowing he would have some kind of memorial, even if it was only a heap of unpaid bills, but facing the possibility of never having existed at all was too much for anybody to . . .

'What's the whole point?' Norman said. 'Go on – you've got me interested.'

'*That's* the point,' Peace replied lamely, his mind racing. 'That I've got you interested. You weren't interested at first, you see. And now you are.'

'So it was a come-on, after all.' The distracted look appeared in Norman's eyes as he took out another bill and placed it beside the first. 'That's twenty you've got – do you mind if we call it quits now?'

Peace made to brush the money aside, then recalled that if he did so it was destined to end up in the hands of the predatory Captain Widget. He lifted the bills and crammed them into his pocket and tried to conceive a new approach to the main problem. Time was rushing by and he was no nearer to learning the guilty secret which was driving Norman, almost literally, to his wit's end.

'Thank you,' he said. 'It goes against the grain for an old legionary like me to accept a handout, but times are hard.'

'Legionary?' Norman looked at him with renewed curiosity. 'But how did you get out?'

'Invalided.' Forgetting the state of his ribs, Peace banged himself on the side of the chest, gave a sharp cry and folded over the table, narrowly avoiding plunging his face into an ashtray.

'Are you all right?' Norman said anxiously.

'Just a twinge.' Peace straightened up, fearful of being evicted by the bartender. 'It's the weather that does it, you know. I'll be all right in a minute.' To cover his confusion he raised his beaker and sipped more coffee.

Norman toyed for a moment with his glass. 'Why did you join up?'

'Ah . . . I wanted to forget something.'

'What was it?'

'How would I know?' Peace could not understand how the conversational roles had become reversed. 'I've forgotten it.'

'Of course – I'm sorry.' Norman nodded, and then – as if something had aroused a painful memory – his lower lip began to tremble.

Peace felt strangely guilty, but he sensed the time was right for him to make a move. 'Norman,' he said gently, 'you're waiting to join the Legion, aren't you?'

'I am! I am! Why don't they open that cursed office? Why do they make us wait so long to lay down our burdens?'

'All in good time,' Peace soothed, glancing around anxiously in case Norman's emotional outburst had disturbed other customers in the bar. 'Listen, Norman, why don't you tell me what's on your mind?'

Norman looked at him with tortured eyes. 'It was a terrible thing I did. I can't talk about it.'

'Of course you can.' Peace placed his free hand over Norman's. 'You can tell me, Norman. Get it off your chest. You'll feel much better.'

'If only that were true.'

'It is. It *is*,' Peace said. 'Tell it to me, Norman.'

'You're sure you really want to hear?'

Peace swallowed nervously. 'I do, Norman. I *do*.'

'All right,' Norman said, in slow, agonized tones. 'My crime is . . .'

'Yes, yes.'

'My crime is . . .'

'Yes, Norman, *yes*!'

'. . . that I deserted from the Legion.'

There came an ear-splitting crash as Peace dropped his coffee beaker on the tiled floor. He gazed strickenly at the top of Norman's bowed head, unable to speak, then found himself dragged to his feet by the bartender, who had vaulted over the counter.

'All right, youse two,' the barman said. 'Outside! I been watching youse two since youse two came in here, and I don't want the likes o' youse two in here.'

'It was an accident, a pure accident.' Peace, his mind still in a downward spiral of disbelief, tucked the twenty monits he had taken from Norman into the barman's shirt pocket and persuaded him to return to his post. The barman gathered up the pieces of ceramic, issued a final warning about holding hands, and shambled away with a number of distrustful backward glances. Peace sat down again and tapped the crown of Norman's head with a single knuckle.

'Look at me, Norman,' he whispered. 'You wouldn't put me on, would you?'

'No. It's the truth.'

'But, *Norman!* Being a deserter from the Legion is nothing to get worked up about. Practically every ranker in the outfit dreams of nothing else. It's their one ambition in life.'

'That's all right for rankers – it's expected of them.' Norman raised his face which was crimson with shame. 'But I was an officer.'

'An officer?' Peace fell silent, trying to fit the new information into the complex puzzle of his life, but Norman had got into his confessional stride and was speaking faster.

'. . . and not just any officer, you see. I was Lieutenant Norman Nightingale, only son of General Nightingale himself. My family has a distinguished record of service in the Legion that goes back two centuries. *Two centuries!* Two hundred years of generals and space marshals, campaigns and courage, medals and honours, glory and greatness. Can you imagine the burden – the unspeakable burden – that tradition placed on me?'

Peace shook his head, partly because it was expected of him, partly because a fierce tingling sensation had developed behind his forehead.

'Almost from the minute I was born, certainly from the cradle, I was prepared and groomed for the Legion. My father never spoke to me about anything else. My *mother* never spoke to me about anything else. My life was totally committed to the Legion – and the terrible thing is that . . . that I had no love for it. I wanted to do other things.' Norman paused, obviously reflecting on his filial short-comings.

Peace was glad of the break because the pins-and-needles had grown stronger, and his memory was throwing up images of a Southern-style white-columned house; a stern-faced, grey-haired man, immaculate in the uniform of a Legion staff officer; a pretty woman, reserved to the point of remoteness, whose upright posture was as militarily correct as that of her husband. These, he knew, were visions of his own childhood, and he began to understand why the memory eraser in the recruiting station had blanked out his entire past. If his whole life had been steeped in the tradition of Space Legion service, his guilt over betraying the family ideal would be equally all-pervading. Every incident stored in his memory, every last detail of his upbringing and early career would be a clue to the nature of his crime – and therefore the machine, with electronic scrupulousness, had deleted the lot.

One of his life's great mysteries had been cleared up, but another had come forward in its place.

'I see the fix you're in, Norman,' Peace said slowly. 'Naturally, with a background like yours, you feel rotten about having gone AWOL – but why go back as a ranker? You don't need to have any memories wiped out – as soon as you return to the Legion you'll cease to be a deserter, and you'll have nothing to feel guilty about. It's as simple as that.'

'As simple as that, he says!' Norman gave a sardonic laugh, indicative of a soul in torment.

'Well, isn't it?'

'If only you knew.'

'For God's sake!' Peace fought back his impatience, remembering that his former self was in dire mental straits. 'Tell me all about it, Norman.'

'The trouble is,' Norman said, gripping his glass in an agitated manner, 'that I didn't just go AWOL. I deserted in the face of the enemy – out of sheer cowardice – and even for a general's son, that's serious.'

'It's pretty serious,' Peace agreed, 'but nothing that our ... your father couldn't square for you.'

Norman shook his head. 'You just don't understand – though, as you haven't had my sort of upbringing, I couldn't expect you to. There's simply no way to wipe out the disgrace I've brought on the family name. In any case, that's not my big problem – it's guilt that's my problem. My own personal, monogrammed, hand-made guilt over the circumstances in which I deserted.'

'Tell me about it,' Peace said, ignoring a clammy touch of unease.

'I can't do that. I don't think I could ever speak to anybody about that.'

This time Norman's reticence made Peace feel relieved rather than angry. 'Okay. So you deserted in the face of the enemy – what happened next?'

Norman took a shaky breath. 'We were fighting on Aspatria at the time. Have you ever been there?'

'Let me see.' Peace pretended to search his memory. 'I think I spent some leave there once.'

'That must have been after the rebellion ended. When I was there in '83 the fighting was still going on, and everything was a bit chaotic. I managed to make my way down to Touchdown City and hide out for a while. The military police were looking for me, of course, but I had no trouble dodging them. It was an easy life for a while, because I had plenty of money – and then some alien beings they call Oscars showed up, and *they* started haunting me. Have you heard about the Oscars?'

A constriction seemed to form around Peace's heart. 'I've heard of them. Why did they come after you?'

'Beats me,' Norman said in a distant voice. 'They just seemed to *know* I'd done something bad – personally I think they can read minds. It was the weirdest thing ever, because it was dark when I first ran into them, and they just seemed to look right inside me with those awful eyes they've got.'

'You say this happened in '83?' Peace frowned as he did some mental juggling with dates. 'But this is 2386 – you don't look like you've been on the run for three years.'

'I haven't.' Norman gave Peace an enigmatic smile. 'But the explanation is so fantastic you'll never believe it.'

'I will. I'll believe anything! Tell it to me, Norman.'

'Well, I'd stayed in my room all day – because usually I only went out at night – and I'd developed quite an appetite, so I decided to have a real blow-out at a sort of restaurant-cum-nightclub called the Blue Toad. It's very expensive, but the food is quite good. Except for the seafood, that is. You'll probably never be there, but if you are, don't order the lobster.'

'I won't,' Peace assured him. 'Was this the night you saw the Oscars?'

'That's what I'm trying to tell you,' Norman reproved. 'I paid for my meal, was given a nasty little souvenir, came out of the restaurant, and as I'd been cooped up in my room all day I decided not to go straight back to it. There was a movie house nearby – one of those multiple projection places – so I went to see what was showing. I had a look at the posters outside, but lost interest when I saw the sort of programme it was. Blatant pornography! Women in the nude!.

'Naturally I didn't want to see anything like that, and

was just about to go somewhere else when – you'll hardly believe this – a boy of about ten approached me and offered me money if I would take him inside and swap strobe-glasses with him. You know, let him see the so-called adult movies.'

'What did you do?' Peace said apprehensively, recalling earlier qualms about his sexual preferences.

'What do you think? I grabbed the brat by the ear and told him I was taking him straight home to his parents.'

'Good for you!' Peace felt a load lift from his mind. 'You did the right thing.'

'That's what I thought, but the evil little swine kicked up a fuss.' A shocked expression appeared on Norman's face as he thought about the incident. 'Would you believe that he told people I'd made certain suggestions to him?'

'My God!'

'It's quite true. He knew exactly what to say – probably makes a habit of hanging around there. Then some manageress woman came out and started shouting at me and blew a whistle. I tell you, it was a ghastly experience. Under the circumstances, being a wanted man and so forth, I decided to get out of there in a hurry, so I made a run for it – and that's when the damned Oscars showed up. I don't know how they managed to appear on the scene so quickly, but two of them made a grab for me, and I only escaped by running up an alley.'

Tingling waves were sweeping over Peace's brain. 'How did you get away from them?'

'This is the really fantastic bit. I thought I could move pretty fast, but the Oscars would have run me into the ground in no time. They'd have caught me if I hadn't noticed a door leading into an old factory building. I shot through it, ran upstairs in the darkness – not knowing where I was – blundered into a toilet, fell over the seat, and . . . you'll never guess what happened next.'

'You went backwards in ti . . .' Peace, who had become carried away with the narrative, cut the fateful word short

Norman looked at him curiously. 'What were you saying?'

'You went backwards. Into the wall.'

'That wasn't what happened at all,' Norman said, annoyed at having his story interrupted at a crucial point. 'Look, do you want to hear this, or don't you?'

'I'm sorry. Please go on.'

'All right – but no more interruptions.'

'I promise.'

'Now, as I was saying – you'll never be able to guess what happened next.'

'I'll never be able to guess,' Peace said dutifully. 'That wasn't an interruption – I was just agreeing with you that I'll never be able to guess.'

'I know you'll never,' Norman said animatedly, 'because the toilet was actually a time machine – an extroverter – and I went backwards in time!'

'My God!'

'It's true! I went right back to the year 2290. The place had just ceased operating as a raincoat factory at that time, but there was a mad character called Legge there who rented an upstairs apartment in it. Funny little man, he was . . . all round and red and rubbery . . . looked like he was constructed from inner tubes. Kept repeating words at the ends of sentences, too, as if there was a ratchet slipping. I didn't take to him much as a person, but I was fascinated by the fact that he was trying to earn a living as an inventor in the electronics field.

'That's the sort of thing I'd always wanted to do, you see. I've got a natural gift for theoretical and applied science, and I can read circuit diagrams the way other people read comic strips, but my family had always made me concentrate on military skills like flying and marksmanship. As far as I could see, Legge had absolutely no talent as an inventor – he was wasting his time trying to build a contraption for making people tell the truth – but he was quick to see that I had some ideas that were worth exploiting, and we formed a kind of partnership. I was almost happy there for a while. I suppose I would actually have *been* happy if it hadn't been for my guilt feelings, and for the presence of Cissy.'

'Was that his daughter?'

'Yes.' Norman looked puzzled again. 'How did you know?'

'Ah . . . mad scientists always have daughters,' Peace said, cursing himself for the verbal slip. 'Pretty little thing, was she?'

'You wouldn't ask that if you'd seen her,' Norman replied fervently, a haunted look appearing in his eyes. 'She kept making advances to me, and I kept fighting her off, and the worst of it was that old Legge had the wrong idea about the whole thing. He was convinced I was some kind of rabid sex maniac who was trying to steal his daughter's virtue right out from under his nose.'

'Funny place to keep it,' Peace said absently.

'Don't be vulgar.' Norman gave him a reproachful glance. 'I hope that service as a ranker won't coarsen me the way it has coarsened you, my friend.'

'I'm sure it won't,' Peace said, making a final vow to keep his mouth shut. 'Go on with the story.'

'As I was saying – I was tortured by memories of my guilt, and it was the same guilt which gave me what I thought was a wonderful idea. I see now that it was a terrible sacrilege, because remorse is a divine scourge. But in my blind arrogance I went ahead and built the infernal machine.'

Peace gripped the edge of the table as instinct and half-formed memory warned him of awful revelations to come. Dark chasms, previously unsuspected, were opening in his mind.

'It took me less than a week to build the prototype of the memory eraser,' Norman continued in a hollow voice.

'My plan was to use it on myself, to cleanse my soul of guilt, and then destroy it – but Legge had plans of his own. I had hardly finished soldering the last connection when he came into the room with one of the pork pies he was always eating and offered me a section. I should have guessed he was up to something, because he was a greedy little brute, and had never given me so much as a crumb before. Ate them straight off a newspaper, he did. Revolting habit! I was always telling him at least to use a plate, but he ...'

Norman stopped speaking as he became aware of the expression on Peace's face. 'I can see from your eyes, my friend, that you've guessed what I'm going to say. Yes, it's quite true – I am the originator of the memory eraser which is used today in every Space Legion recruiting station throughout the inhabited galaxy!'

Peace shook his head and gripped Norman's wrist, trying to stem the flow of words, but to no avail.

'The pork pie was drugged, of course,' Norman continued, 'and as soon as I became groggy that fiend Legge hustled me downstairs, opened the toilet door – a *female* toilet door, I might add – and threw me inside. I fell on to the seat, and the next thing I knew I was in the Touchdown City of 2386. I had overshot my departure point in time by three years – the time machine must have been in a phase of increasing oscillations.'

'Not damping oscillations,' Peace said numbly.

'I said increasing oscillations, didn't I?' The momentary irritation faded from Norman's face. 'I'm sorry – I realize I've given you quite a shock. You never expected to meet face to face with the man who invented the very machine which was used on you when you joined up, did you?'

'Not really,' Peace murmured.

'Of course, you didn't. Perhaps now you can imagine how I felt when I learned the truth. At first I was quite pleased at finding myself in 2386 – the fighting was over, and the military police seemed to have forgotten about me. I was curious to discover what Legge had been up to, so I went to a newspaper office and looked through their old files. They're all on microfilm, of course – I was told the actual old newspapers are worth their weight in diamonds – so it was easy to turn up a complete biography on Legge.'

'What did it say?'

'That he had died in 2321, rich and famous as the inventor of the Space Legion's memory eraser. There were no other inventions to his credit, which proves the little toad had no talent, but he'd even been given a science chair at the Aspatrian Military Academy on the strength of the eraser. Professor Legge, can you imagine? Huh!'

'Wait a minute.' Peace was desperately trying to ground himself in new realities. 'You can't blame yourself for the memory eraser. I mean it was in widespread use in 2383, and you must have known about it before you went back in time, so . . .'

'That doesn't change anything. I'd heard about the eraser, naturally, but I didn't know when it was invented. And when I got back to 2290 I was too wrapped up in my own selfish schemes to check around and find that the device was unknown at that time. Legge must have been bowled over when I proposed the idea, but he was too cunning to let me see that. He bears some responsibility, of course, but I was the prime mover – I am the arch-criminal.'

'You invented a machine to alleviate mental suffering,' Peace argued. 'That wasn't a criminal act.'

'Wasn't it?' Norman's lips twisted in a wan smile. 'What use has that machine been put to? Thousands of young men are lured into the Legion by the promise of forgetfulness – and what happens to them? They get killed. They die young – and now I can't even pretend it's in a good cause.

'I was brought up to believe that the Legion exemplified everything that is fine and noble in our society. When I was a small child I used to dream about crusading through the galaxy in a tall golden ship – not realizing that the Legion's chief function is to force people on other worlds to buy Earth's surplus production of television sets and electric toothbrushes.'

'This is terrible,' Peace quavered, feeling the onset of a gloom which made his former state of mind seem enviable.

'It's all right for you,' Norman said. 'Try to imagine how *I* feel, knowing that I'm so much to blame. I know I should try to live with my guilt, accept the punishment I brought down on myself, but I just can't go on like this any longer. As soon as I learned the full extent of what I'd done in the past, and added it to what I'd done in the present, I realized there was only one thing to do – join the Legion. To forget. Ironic, isn't it?'

'You're telling me,' Peace said. His head was throbbing violently with the pain of recaptured memory. Virtually his whole past was accessible to him now, and it was worse than he had feared, but most frightening of all was the realization that there was one depth he had yet to plumb. There was a black hole, a Stygian well of guilt and horror, beckoning to him. Norman had refused to discuss it, but the corrosive stains of memory were spreading into every compartment of Peace's mind . . .

'That was two days ago,' Norman was saying. 'I didn't want to try joining the Legion on Aspatria because there was too big a risk of somebody there recognizing me, so I bought a ticket to Earth.'

'You didn't run into any Oscars?'

'Not this time. I was lucky.' Norman touched the wood of the table. 'Perhaps they were too busy hounding some other poor sod – if so, I feel sorry for him.'

Peace nodded, scarcely listening. Two names had sprung into his mind – Ozzy Drabble and Hec Magill. Associated with the unusual names were two faces. They were thin, weather-beaten faces, stamped with the rueful expression of the Space Legion ranker, but they also contained individuality and humour. Those faces, he knew, had been important to him at some stage of his life – and there was only one slot into which they could be fitted. They had to be part of the mystery surrounding his desertion in the face of the enemy.

The veils surrounding that incident were steadily being drawn aside by the forces at work inside his brain, and Peace shuddered with apprehension as he realized there was nothing he could do now to forestall the final revelation.

'Listen, Norman,' he said, seeking distraction, 'aren't you worried about anybody in the recruiting office guessing who you are? I mean, Nightingale is one of the most famous names in the Legion.'

Norman shook his head. 'I've already taken care of that. I'm changing my name to Leo Tolstoy.'

'Tolstoy?' Peace blinked at him in surprise.

'Yes. He's my favourite among the great Russian authors, and I'm in a gloomy Russian mood, so it seems an appropriate choice.'

'But . . . How does this name-changing business work?'

Norman glanced over his shoulder to make sure there were no unwanted listeners. 'Lots of people who want to shake off their pasts change their names when they join the Legion. But you can't just give a false name when you go in, because the Legion medics put you into an hypnotic trance for the memory erasure and electro-psycho response

163

conditioning, and in that state you wouldn't respond to the alias.'

'So what do you do?'

'You go to a professional name-changer, which is another way of saying you go to a hypnotist who implants your chosen alias under deep hypnosis. It's an illegal practice, of course, but you usually find one or two specialists in that sort of thing near every recruiting station. There's one just along the block from here. Tomlinson, you call him – he operates under cover of being a barber, but I think he makes most of his money out of hypnotizing fugitives. That's where I'm going in a few minutes – it's all set up.' Norman rubbed a small clear patch in the condensation on the window beside him and peered out.

'I think I saw some lights go on over in the fort. I'd better be on my way.'

'Wait a minute,' Peace said, reluctant to be left alone with his thoughts, and still puzzled about the discrepancy in names. 'Are you sure nothing can go wrong during the name-changing operation?'

'Thinking of going through it yourself, eh?' Norman gave Peace a speculative stare. 'There's no need to worry about anything going wrong – Tomlinson says his system is foolproof. He does the hypnosis with a machine. The way it works is that you print the name you want to have on a piece of paper, and you just keep staring at it while the machine puts you into the right sort of trance. It couldn't be simpler.'

'Have you got your new name written down?'

'I've gone one better – I've got it *printed*, in big letters, so that my mind can't wander.' Norman took a thick paperback novel out of his jacket pocket and tapped it with his finger. 'It's right here on the front of this book.'

'Are you sure that's a good idea?' Peace said, wondering

if he was wise to interfere. 'I mean, you might stare at the wrong part of the book. Sort of accidentally.'

'What a silly suggestion! I'm not going to christen my-self War And Peace, am I?'

'I meant accidentally.'

'I'm rather accident prone, my friend, but not to that extent.' Norman stood up with an air of finality, put his book away and extended his hand to Peace. 'It wasn't fair of me to burden a complete stranger with all my worries – but thanks for being such a good listener.'

'It's all right.' Peace shook his hand. 'Perhaps you'll do the same for me some day.'

'I doubt if our paths will ever cross again,' Norman said. He went out of the bar and a few seconds later his blurred outline – moving at a funereal pace appropriate to its load of care – passed across the misted window and was lost to view.

Peace stared for a moment at the blank grey screen of glass, and suddenly his imagination illuminated it with a scene from another world and another time. He pressed both hands to his temples as, amid a crescendo of pain, his memory was made complete, and he knew the full, un-speakable extent of his shame.

chapter eleven

Lieutenant Norman Nightingale was leading a foot patrol through the forests of the Aspatrian high country, a hun-dred kilometres north of Touchdown City.

He was advancing with extreme caution, carrying his

radiation rifle at the ready, prepared to burn anything which made a sudden move. His willingness to shoot was inspired by the desire to remain alive, coupled with the knowledge that, in this area, he would not be called upon to fire at human beings. Nightingale had no stomach for fighting the Aspatrian colonists, whose claim for independence he regarded as being fully justified.

He had acquired some local knowledge during his brief stay on the planet, and he knew that the native Aspatrians never went into the high forests, not even for military expedience. The overhanging boughs were the home of the strange omnivorous creatures, which – because of their blanket-like shape and patterned colouration – had been dubbed throwrugs by the rankers. The homely term was perhaps meant to disguise the dread and loathing the men had for an enemy which pounced without warning, could not be shaken off, and brought a death which was spectacularly nasty, even by Legion standards. Any man who saw a comrade fall victim to a throwrug was required to shoot him immediately, and those who had been through such incidents – far from regarding this as a harsh measure – made their fellow soldiers vow to give them the same treatment, should the need arise.

Nightingale's mind was in a turmoil as he picked his way through the sun-dappled silence of the forest. He disliked service life in general, and particularly resented the arbitrariness of the staff order to clean the Aspatrians out of a forest which the Aspatrians were too prudent to have entered in the first place. Adding to his anger and concern was the fact that he was accompanied by two good men – Ozzy Drabble and Hec Magill – whose lives were his responsibility. He regarded the pair as friends despite the sharp officer-ranker schism of the Legion's structure. His regiment, the 81st, was a crack outfit in which the use of command enforcer implants was scorned, which would

*have made it possible for veteran legionaries to have given
a rough passage to an inexperienced young lieutenant. But
he had always had loyalty and unobtrusive moral support
from Drabble and Magill, and was desperately anxious
that no harm should befall them on his account.*

*They were moving line abreast, with Nightingale in
the centre, when the first throwrug struck.*

*Nightingale heard the soft impact and muffled screams
on his right. He spun and saw Magill falling to the ground,
his body enveloped in the predator's terrible bright folds.
The legionary began to writhe as the fronds wrapped
themselves around his body and the digestive secretions
went to work on his flesh. Nightingale stared at the scene
in horror, totally unable to move.*

*'Out of the way, Lieutenant,' Drabble shouted from the
left. 'I can't hit him without burning you as well.'*

*Nightingale turned just in time to see the second throw-
rug claim Drabble, who had levelled his rifle and was trying to get into position for a mercy shot. Drawn into a
tight ball, the creature fell like a stone until it was a short
distance above Drabble's head, then it unfolded in the last
instant to cloak his entire body. He went down without a
sound, but the violence of his struggles was an eloquent
plea for Nightingale to perform the ultimate act of
comradeship.*

*His lips moving silently, Nightingale tried to take aim.
And there came the sound of movement in the branches
above him.*

*He threw down his rifle and fled, continuing to run —
like a man pursued by demons — long after he had reached
the safety of open ground.*

Peace gazed for many minutes into the spurious grey
depths of the misted window, knowing that he had at last
reached the end of the trail, that the pilgrimage was over.

He had learned exactly who he was, he had learned exactly *what* he was – and the knowledge was such that he could not bear to live with it. The burden of guilt was too great.

There's only one thing for it, he thought, struggling to his feet. *'I'll have to join the Space Legion. To forget.'*

He was in poor physical condition, but the Legion's recruiting officers were so anxious to make up their quotas that they would accept anybody who could be repaired without recourse to major surgery. By the same token, they rarely queried the identity of recruits or investigated their past lives, but – as had been pointed out to him – he was going to need a new name. His family's prominence in the Legion meant he could not call himself Norman Nightingale, and there were unacceptable hazards associated with trying to become Leo Tolstoy.

'Not risking going in as Anna Karenina,' Peace muttered in his beard. 'Things were bad enough the first two times round with men's names.' He went to the bar counter, obtained a scrap of paper, deliberated for a moment, then wrote in large block letters the name: JUDAS FINK.

Gloomily satisfied with the appellation, he shoved the paper into his pocket and made his way to the door, but hesitated before going through it, reluctant to face the coldness and hostility of the world outside. Several seconds went by before he appreciated the full irrationality of his fears – after what he had been through, the future, any future, simply had to be an improvement.

He opened the door and walked out of the bar – and found himself face to face with the two Oscars.

The brazen giants moved instantaneously to bar his way, hemming him into the small entrance hall, and he knew that on this occasion – barring a miracle – there could be no escape.

He was raising his hands in surrender, when a passable

imitation of a miracle occurred. His other self, Norman Nightingale, his business at the name-changer's place presumably completed, came into view a short distance away and crossed the street towards the shabby hulk of Fort Eccles. Oblivious to his surroundings, eyes fixed steadfastly on the ground, Nightingale dragged himself dejectedly up the short flight of stone steps and passed through the doors of the recruiting office.

The Oscars watched him disappear, then their heads slowly turned until they were looking into each other's slitted ruby eyes. They froze in that position, and Peace could have sworn their smooth-cast features were registering surprise and bafflement. Seizing the heaven-sent opportunity, he ducked beneath the outspread arms and scuttled to freedom. A lancing pain in his ribs made running difficult, but there was the inevitable entrance to an alley only a few paces away, and he threw himself into it with a sob of gratitude.

The truck which was coming out of the alley at that precise instant hit him hard.

Peace bounced into the roadway and lay perfectly still, staring at the sky. He knew there was no point in trying to do anything more constructive, because he had felt the snap of bones, and a subtle wrongness within his body hinted at other damage. In the murmurous distance he heard the truck driver begin to protest his innocence, and to fall silent as the Oscars appeared on the immediate scene.

They leaned over Peace, shuttering the sky with massive shoulders, their faces unreadable. One of them slid his arms under him and lifted, and the agony this movement occasioned told him his life was drawing to a close. The long pilgrimage had, indeed, ended.

There followed a confused period, a lapse into a discontinuous universe in which events were plotted against the all-important dimension of pain, and in which consciousness came and went with the ponderous regularity of night and day. He was faintly aware of high-speed movement through city streets . . . of discovering that an Oscar's skin was warm and not, as he had expected, cold . . . of the clang of heavy metal doors like those of a ship . . . of expanding patterns of stars on a black screen, suns hurtling by at unthinkable multitudes of the speed of light . . . a glimpse from space of a green-and-white world which could have been Aspatria . . . dancing, shifting traceries of light and shade which, by dint of great effort, he recognized as a canopy of branches . . . the branches of the trees . . . the branches of the trees of the forest . . . the branches of the trees of the forests of the Aspatrian uplands . . .

'Oh, *no*!' Peace tried to scream, overwhelmed by a night-black tide of premonition, but he was unable to form the words. And hard on the heels of his despair came a kind of acceptance, a belated understanding that he could achieve lasting rest only by enduring what he had caused others to endure.

The Oscars were avenging angels, cool administrators of divine justice, and for that he should be grateful to them – because, more than he craved life itself, he longed to be at peace with his conscience.

He lay quietly on the leaf-strewn ground, watched the Oscars bring a throwrug to him, and was almost smiling as its living fronds – blood-red underside alive with a million tiny feelers – descended hungrily on to his face and broken body.

chapter twelve

Much though he had always hoped for a life after death, Warren Peace had not expected it to come so quickly.

He sat up – feeling impossibly strong, impossibly good – and glanced down in wonderment at his gleaming new body. It was an heroic Michelangelo sculpture brought to life, a visual symphony of power, proportion and beauty. Highlights flickered across his golden skin as he stood up with a single lithe movement and looked about him.

There was no sign of the throwrug, but the two Oscars who had administered it to him were standing nearby, smiling. He experienced no fear, because he understood he was now one of their kind, and with his acute new vision he perceived that their faces were not as alike as he had once believed. Each had an individuality, a distinct identity which was strangely familiar ...

'It's you two!' he cried disbelievingly. 'Ozzy Drabble and Hec Magill!'

'That's right, Norman,' Drabble said coming forward. 'I wish you had recognized us a bit sooner – it would have saved an awful lot of running about.'

'But I thought you were *dead*!'

'A natural mistake, I suppose,' Magill put in. 'Everybody thought the throwrugs were trying to eat people – not to go into symbiotic partnership with them – and I guess it did look pretty frightening.'

Drabble nodded. 'Thanks to you, Norman, Hec and I were the first human beings who didn't get shot before the process was completed. We owe you a lot. The human race owes you a lot.'

'It was only because I was too afraid,' Peace confessed. 'I was too much of a ...'

'Don't think about it,' Drabble said. 'You're an Oscar now, and you'll never feel fear again. The throwrug has melded itself into your body – that accounts for the extra mass – and into your nervous system. You're a superman now, Norman.'

'But – for God's sake! – why didn't you *tell* somebody? Why didn't you let people know the true situation instead of going around frightening everybody to death?'

Drabble looked apologetic. 'Well, we've got subetheric voices and hearing now. We can talk to each other even when we're thousands of kilometres apart, but ordinary human ears can't hear us. Even dogs can't hear us. Somebody like you could probably build a speech converter so that we could talk to humans, but we're not so sure that would be a good idea.'

'Why not?'

'Because we don't frighten *everybody*,' Magill said. 'The ordinary law-abiding citizens got used to us very quickly – it's only the crooks, the bad guys, who take sick when they see us around. And it's because they know they can't hide from us, and we can't be bought off or fought off. Maybe that's not a bad thing, Norman. Maybe the human race needs somebody like us.'

Peace frowned at him. 'Isn't that setting ourselves up rather high?'

'We *are* rather high – in fact, we're the highest,' Magill replied, unabashed. 'Partnership with a throwrug develops your ethical sense even more than it improves your body. Ozzy and I, with a handful of other legionaries we managed to convert before they would have died from wounds, stopped the war right here on Aspatria. Think how many lives we saved by doing that.

'We're symbiotic supermen, Norman – untroubled by human weaknesses such as the need for food, water, heat, air, even sex – and with your help we're going to spread out through the galaxy, stopping wars, stamping out crime and corruption everywhere we go. Just think of it, Norman – isn't that the sort of life you've always really wanted?'

Peace considered the proposition for a moment, and realized that Magill's words were perfectly true. He gazed at his two companions, his slow-dawning smile mirrored on their golden faces, and the purest happiness he had ever known fountained through his inner being.

He extended his hands, Drabble and Magill linked arms with him, and – singing at the tops of their subetheric voices – the three gleaming giants danced away through the forest, playfully kicking down the occasional tree in their unbounded exuberance.

Bob Shaw
Medusa's Children 70p

The Clan live in a strange undersea world of nets and metal objects
anchored to a giant plant. This is the Home and outside it lie the hazards
of the deep. Now their environment is slowly changing. A new current
is growing daily stronger and flowing downwards, drawing, drawing
everything down towards the realm of the mysterious deity, Ka . . .

Cosmic Kaleidoscope 70p

From the prize-winning author of *Orbitsville*, nine stories which
demonstrate Shaw's superb imaginative range and cynically humorous
approach to the world of the future.

'There's an SF Western, a kind of futuristic Chandler and a comic-strip
horror story . . . After Ballard himself, Bob Shaw is the nearest we've
got to a home-grown Great' OBSERVER

A Wreath of Stars 70p

Thornton's Planet is an anti-neutrino planet whose appearance causes
a wave of panic . . . then comes news from the African state of Barandi;
miners wearing magniluct lenses have seen ghosts in the mine
passages . . . the passage of Thornton's Planet has had further-reaching
effects on Earth than anyone could have imagined . . .

'Shaw is improving with everything he does . . . the most accomplished
of the younger British stable' OBSERVER

Christopher Priest
Indoctrinaire 75p

'A novelist of real distinction' THE TIMES

In a laboratory deep under the Antarctic, Wentik is experimenting
with mind-affecting drugs. Suddenly he is transported into the
22nd-century Brazilian jungle. After nuclear war only South America
has survived, but vestiges of the war gases remain to create 'The
Disturbances' and threaten the social order. Wentik must return to his
own time to find out about the gas and its antidote . . . but finds himself
in the wrong time-slot, and the war has already begun . . .

'Excellent . . . a Kafke-type nightmare' SUNDAY TIMES

A Dream of Wessex 75p

'His imaginative construction of a 22nd-century Wessex which has been
separated from the mainland by catastrophic earthquakes. Dorchester
has become a big tourist centre with mosques and casinos . . . A very
clever novel' THE LISTENER

Fugue for a Darkening Island 70p

'Britain in the near future. In power is a strong right-wing Government
struggling against rising prices and unemployment. Then the African
refugees begin to arrive . . .' SUNDAY EXPRESS

'In the Wyndham tradition; but Wyndham's mellow sunsets have faded
and the dark night of the soul is coming down'
BRIAN ALDISS, GUARDIAN

Robert Silverberg
Downward to the Earth 75p

The planet Belzagor is predominantly jungle, populated with bizarre flora and fauna, governed by the elephant-like alien *nildoror*, and the bi-pedal *sulidoror*. Gundersen was last on Belzagor when it was a colonial planet and he was an administrator; now he returns to meet old friends. But Gundersen is still driven by an old guilt, and he needs to undergo the bizarre *nildor* rite of 'rebirth' for his own metamorphosis...

'Probably the most intelligent SF writer in America' URSULA LE GUIN

Robert Holdstock
Earthwind 80p

'On the planet Aeran, the original colonists have undergone a drastic change: under the influence of some strange psychic force they have forgotten their identity and created a new culture – an exact reconstruction of the Stone Age society that flourished in Ireland 6,000 years ago... An absorbing and thought-provoking mystery tinged with mysticism' OXFORD TIMES

Brian Stableford
The Fenris Device 60p

On an inhospitable planet where no man has ventured before lies the wreck of a Gallacellan warship – the vehicle of the oldest spacefaring race in the galaxy. Aboard the wreck is a legendary weapon – The Fenris Device... a legend strong enough to attract the masters of the *Hooded Swan* in their thirst for knowledge.

You can buy these and other Pan books from booksellers and newsagents; or direct from the following address:
Pan Books, Sales Office, Cavaye Place, London SW10 9PG
Send purchase price plus 20p for the first book and 10p for each additional book to allow for postage and packing
Prices quoted are applicable in the UK

While every effort is made to keep prices low, it is sometimes necessary to increase prices at short notice. Pan Books reserve the right to show on covers and charge new retail prices which may differ from those advertised in the text or elsewhere